Harold and Bella, Jammy and Me

Our gang, Harold and Bella, Jammy and me, was always getting into some scrape or other: playing Hallowe'en tricks on the Tunnel Top gang . . .; coming home soaked after we'd found the bridge over the stream up in the woods, and the other lot happened to come along . . .; investigating the caves where we'd heard King Arthur and his knights still slept . . .

Full of colourful characters and humorous adventures, this is a vivacious collection of stories about a group of children growing up in a Northern town.

Other Fontana Lions books by Robert Leeson

Grange Hill Rules – OK?
Grange Hill Goes Wild
Grange Hill for Sale
Grange Hill Home and Away
Forty Days of Tucker J.
The Third Class Genie
Genie on the Loose
'Maroon Boy
Bess
The White Horse
Silver's Revenge
Beyond the Dragon Prow

And for younger readers

Challenge in the Dark
The Demon Bike Rider

Robert Leeson

Harold and Bella, Jammy and Me

FONTANA LIONS
ORIGINAL

For Marie, Edna and Phil

First published in Fontana Lions 1980
8 Grafton Street, London W1X 3LA
Fourth impression November 1986

Fontana Lions is an imprint of
Fontana Paperbacks, part of
the Collins Publishing Group

Made and printed in Great Britain by
William Collins Sons & Co. Ltd, Glasgow

Contents

Jammy

We had four in our gang in Tarcroft, Jammy and Harold and Bella and me. Jammy's real name was Alan but we never called him anything else but Jammy. Why? Because whatever he did turned out right – for him. He always had jam on it, so we called him Jammy.

If you saw something shiny lying in the gutter on your way to school and picked it up, yours would be an old glass bottle washer. If Jammy saw something it would be a big marble all the colours of the rainbow, a real bobby dazzler.

If it was acorn time and you were trying to make a flop gun out of a piece cut from an old elder branch, yours would split the first time you shoved the firing stick down it. Jammy's would be firm and smooth, bound with cord, solid as a rock. When he spat on the stick and drew it down the barrel, it would go 'flop' like a gun. When he fired it, the acorn would shoot out of the end like a rocket. When you asked him how he managed it, he'd grin in a daft way and say 'Dad did it'. At home his garden and back was full of old rubbish and his Dad was always mending and fixing things.

At school, if you were passing notes in class and teacher found out, the note would be in your hands, not his, even if he wrote it.

He never got measles or chicken pox or whooping cough. But he would always stop home when you got them because he'd been out with you when you caught them.

Don't ask me how he did it. Some people are made like that. He was so lucky it was sickening. He was cheeky with it, too. But I liked him, he was a good mate.

And bets – he always won bets. Never bet with Jammy, we always said. He's too jammy. But we always ended up taking him on. The odds were so tempting.

This day we were out bike riding. Well, we were out with our bikes. We had two bikes between us. Jammy had an old cronk which his Dad had found somewhere and fixed up. The frame must have been made for a six-year-old and the saddle was raised so high Jammy looked like a circus performer perched up in the air.

Harold had a new bike for his birthday with a BSA three speed to get you uphill. I wished I had a three speed. I wished I had a bike to put it on. I expect Bella did too, but she didn't say anything. She put up with a lot, did Bella. She was Harold's sister and he was always bossing her about. But more often than not she'd just wrinkle up her nose and throw back her hair out of her eyes, then make a face at Harold, behind his back.

The man who invented the three speed must have been thinking of our place, because Tarcroft is built on a hill. They called it 'The City on the Hill', and Mr Bagwell who preached in Chapel on Sundays used to say: 'A city that is built upon a hill cannot be hid.'

Lots of people thought Tarcroft ought to be hidden or wiped off the map. In fact most of the maps don't even show it. But it was there all right. It sat on the top of this ridge like a little fort, with the river running round the bottom like a moat. Half way down the hill the canal curved round. Anyone who wanted to attack it would have had their work cut out. But nobody tried.

When you went for a bike ride, you started off with a bang. Downhill, it was smashing, round the bend, over the canal bridge, down past the woods and the water meadows, then sharp right over the river bridge. Until they put traffic lights there, when we got traffic, you could ride down and across the river without pedalling. But then you had to traipse all the way back up the hill, pushing your bike and thinking, was it worth it? Even Harold's new bike wouldn't take you all the way.

We were standing at the top of our road one day, admiring Harold's bike, when Bella said:

'Wouldn't it be lovely, if there was a bike ride where you could free-wheel all the way?'

'Tell you what,' I said. 'What if they had estimators in different places, so you could free-wheel down and then get a lift up again!'

'Estimator? You daft onk,' interrupted Harold. 'You mean escalator'. He always knew better.

'No, he doesn't,' said Jammy, 'he means a shee-lift like they have in Switzerland.'

'It's not shee-lift, it's ski-lift.'

' 'Tisn't.'

'Want to bet?'

'Oh, give over you lot, you give me a headache,' said Bella. 'Let's go to the Clough.'

We set off. I rode on Jammy's crossbar and Bella tucked her frock up and climbed on Harold's carrier.

'Gerroff,' he snapped, 'that'll never hold your weight. Get on the crossbar.'

'What and have that three speed sticking in me –?'

'Oh, come on,' said Jammy, 'race you to the Clough.'

He didn't bet this time. He was crafty. He knew Harold would beat him on that new bike. When Jammy and I rode up, they were waiting for us at the top of the Clough.

The Clough was a big hollow on the other side of Tarcroft with trees on either side and a stream running through under the road at the bottom. Some people reckoned it had a gradient of one in three going down and one in two going up the other side. If you wanted to reach the top without getting off and pushing, then you had to pedal like mad all the way down, and keep pedalling right up the slope. It was tricky because right at the foot of the slope the road swerved to the right.

'Come on,' said Jammy. 'Let's see who can get to the top without pedalling, standing start.'

'You're off your rocker. It can't be done.'

'Want to bet?' asked Jammy.

'Let's see you do it.'

'You'll never do that in a month of Sundays, Jammy,' I said.

'Want to bet?' asked Jammy.

'How much?'

'Three to one.'

'What, all of us?'

'Yes, you're all on.'

'What in? Washers?'

'No, threepenny joey to a penny.'

'You're crackers,' we said. Threepence was a week's pocket money at least.

'Want to bet?' He wasn't giving in. He wheeled his

old bike into the middle of the road. We followed.

'Ready?'

He nodded and clenched his teeth. We gave him a good push off, it seemed only fair. After all, he was going to be ruined. He'd have to sell all his marbles and next season's conkers before he was done. And away he went downhill, pedalling like mad, no brakes, not even a touch. He was picking up speed every inch of the way, and must have been doing nearly fifty when he reached the bend at the foot of the hollow.

'Don't forget – free-wheel up the other side,' yelled Harold.

Jammy never heard him, because just as he shot into the rise, his saddle, which his Dad had fixed, came loose and cocked right up till he was nearly sitting on his own back mud-guard. He lost control, swerved like mad, flew over the tarmac, left the road, burst clean through the hedge and vanished.

'You've lost this time, Jammy,' shouted Harold. But there was no answer.

'Hey up, he's hurt himself,' said Bella.

'Never.'

Bella started running downhill, calling 'Jammy'. I ran after and Harold jumped on his bike and came too. At the bottom we looked through the hedge. Jammy lay on his back in the nettles and dock leaves. His bike, the wheels twisted round, lay in the stream. His eyes were closed.

'We'll have to get the ambulance man,' said Bella.

'Doctor, you dope,' snapped Harold. He jumped back on his bike and pedalled off up the Clough. Luckily he met the doctor on his rounds and down he came in his car. We helped lift Jammy into the back seat. His eyes were open now, but he didn't say a word. The doctor looked at us.

'How did this happen?'

'It was a bet –' I began.

'You ought to be ashamed of yourselves, daring him to do a silly prank like this.'

We were speechless.

'Still, he's not too badly off. Touch of shock. I'll take him home and you can call round and see him tomorrow.'

We picked up Jammy's bike, straightened the wheels and took it home. Next day, we clubbed together, bought some spanish, the sort that's wrapped round in a big roll with a toffee in the middle, and the latest *Hotspur* comic, and called round at Jammy's. His mother let us up to the bedroom where he was lying, looking weak. When he saw us, his face lit up. He held out his hand.

'Come on, pay up.'

'Pay up? What's the big idea?'

'That bet, three to one. You lost. I won.'

'What d'you mean? You came off, half way,' spluttered Harold.

Jammy smiled like a cat in the cream.

'Did I, or did I not, get up the Clough without pedalling?'

We looked at him and then at each other.

'Well, you jammy ha'porth!' we said.

Harold

Harold was a show off. Whatever you knew, he knew better. Whatever you had, he had better. And he could always win the argument by thumping you, because he was bigger. That was the main reason why we put up with him. Because the gang in the street round the corner from us would have slaughtered us if it hadn't been for Harold. With him around we could slog 'em any time. So, even when he gave you the pip, which was about ten times a day, you put up with him.

As I said, whatever was going new, his family had to have it first – sliced bread, gate-legged tables, copper fire irons, zip fasteners. They had rubber hot water bottles when the rest of us still had a hot brick in an old sock, a gas cooker when our Mams still cooked on the open range, an electric iron when Mam still heated her iron on the fire and spat on it to test the heat. They were first to have a five-shilling flip in a monoplane at Blackpool and they were first to have the telephone put in round our way. That was a dead loss because there was almost no one to ring up. It was sickening all round, the way they carried on. But worst of all was when they got the wireless.

Mr Marconi's invention was slow to arrive in Tarcroft. That is if you didn't count the crystal sets owned by the doctor and the man who hired out the charabanc. Most people couldn't afford the wireless at first. But, of course, when Mr Marconi did arrive round our way, he came to Harold's house first.

We were sitting, the four of us, one day in the branches of the old oak tree that stands in the Meadows at the top of the Lane, when Harold spoke up:

'We're getting a wireless.'

There was silence for a second or two. What could you say? Then, just as Harold was going to speak again, Jammy said:

'So are we.'

'Get off. You're a little ligger, Jammy.'

'Am not.'

'Are.'

'Want to bet?' asked Jammy, and he stretched himself out along his branch with hands behind his head, lying balanced. I don't know how he dared do it, twenty feet up.

'Want to bet?' he repeated.

Harold kept his mouth shut a minute, then burst out:

'All right, what make is it?'

'Cossor.'

'They're no good. Ours is a Phillips.'

'Get off. Cossor are better than Phillips any day.'

'Not.'

'Are.'

Bella made a face at me. Harold went on.

'Our wireless pole's twenty-five foot high.'

'Ours is thirty foot,' said Jammy.

'It never.'

' 'Tis 'n' all.'

'How d'you know?'

'Because our Dad climbed it when he fixed the aerial.'

Harold laughed like a drain.

'I always knew you were a monkey – that proves it.'

Jammy retorted : 'I bet your Dad couldn't climb the clothes post.'

'My Dad wouldn't mess about climbing a wireless pole like a chimpanzee. We had a man in to fix ours. I bet your Dad didn't buy a wireless. Bet he put it together with bits and pieces.'

That was getting near the mark. Jammy's Dad was always fixing things.

'He never,' said Jammy, but he looked a bit funny.

'OK,' went on Harold. 'Bet you can't get Radio Luxemburg.'

'Can a duck swim ? Course we can.'

'All right. What do you listen in to ?'

'Ovaltineys.'

'They're no good. Joe the Sanpic Man's miles better.'

'Him ? He's barmy, like you.'

'You're crackers.'

'You two give me a headache,' snapped Bella. But Harold wouldn't give up.

'How big's your wireless cabinet ?' he asked craftily.

'How big's yours ?' asked Jammy.

'Ya ha,' sneered Harold. 'You daren't say because ours is bigger and you know it.'

'Want to bet ?' said Jammy. But I had a feeling he was getting desperate.

'OK. How much ?' Harold was sure of himself and I began to feel sorry for Jammy.

'Ten to one.' Jammy was getting wild now.

'What in, conkers ?'

'No, tanners.'

'You never, that's a dollar if you lose.'

Bella climbed down to a lower branch, hung on for

a moment with her hands, then dropped to the ground.
  'I'm off.'

I jumped down after her and Jammy followed. He
was mad. Harold was laughing at him and I knew
Jammy was making it up. Next day, though, we all
went down to the Clough and played sliding in the old
sandpit. It was smashing. I thought the stupid bet had
been forgotten. I hated quarrels and so did Bella. But
Harold hadn't forgotten at all.

Next week, Bella came round after school. That
Wednesday there was to be a wedding in the Royal
Family. School was closed for a half day. Would we like
to come round and listen to it on their wireless? I
thought to myself, Harold's Mam's as bad as he is.

When we got round there on the day, there was
quite a crowd in their front room. Jammy's mother
was there and some other women from our street and
even one from round the corner.

She wore a funny big hat and had a put-on accent.

'Oh, I see you've had your sofa covered in rexine.'

'Oh, yes,' said Harold's Mam, 'it's the latest thing for
settees.' She said the word 'settee' a bit louder, but the
other woman didn't seem to notice.

'I'm not sure I fancy rexine, myself, it makes your
drawers stick to your bottom.'

'Would you care for a cup of tea?' Harold's Mam
said quickly to our Mam, who was staring out of the
window to hide a smile.

While all this was going on, Harold was nudging
Jammy and pointing to the corner. There on a special
table stood the wireless, a big brown walnut cabinet
with ornamental carving over the loudspeaker part and
a line of polished buttons along the bottom. I thought

Jammy looked sick. That wireless was enormous. It must have been two feet high and a foot across. Harold's mother switched on. There was a lot of crackling and spitting.

'Just atmospherics,' she said

Jammy looked more cheerful. Perhaps it wouldn't work. But it did. Harold's mother gave the cabinet a very unladylike thump on the top and the crackling stopped. We could hear an organ playing and an old bloke droning on about something, then some singing, then a lot more crackling. Another hefty bang on the top and we heard a bloke with a posh voice telling us what we'd been listening to, in case we hadn't got it. I didn't think much to it all, but Mam and the other women said it was lovely. Then Jammy's mother piped up.

'On Saturday afternoon, I'd like you all round to our house for a cup of tea. There's a nice music programme we can listen in to.'

Harold's mother looked a bit peeved but smiled and said : 'Delighted.' But Jammy looked green. Harold sniggered and whispered, 'That'll cost you a dollar.'

When we got outside I said : 'Hey, Harold, this bet's daft. Jammy hasn't got a dollar. It'll take him months to save that up.'

Bella nodded. But Harold smirked.

'Serve him right. He should keep his big mouth shut.' He turned round and swung on the gate. 'See you on Saturday, Jammy – have the money ready. I'll take two half dollars, or five bobs, ten tanners or twenty three-penny joeys. But not sixty pennies, 'cause it weighs your pockets down.'

Jammy slouched off down the road by himself.

Saturday tea time came round all too soon and there we were in Jammy's kitchen. They didn't have a front room. Jammy's mother had a good fire going, though it was the middle of July, and the kettle was boiling. The table was loaded with bread and butter, meat paste and corned beef sandwiches, and scones. We all sat down. Harold looked all round him, a fat grin on his face.

'Where's the wireless, Missis?'

'You speak when you're spoken to,' said his Mam.

'That's quite all right,' said Jammy's Mam. 'Alan, just take the dust cloth off will you, love.'

Jammy nipped sharply up from the table and whipped away a cloth that was hanging in the corner. I heard Harold choke on a mouthful of bread and butter. We all stared as Jammy switched on and the music came through with hardly any crackling.

But the cabinet! It must have been five foot high, not on a table, but standing on the floor. The loud-speaker part was decorated with cream-coloured scroll work. Below were two sets of knobs and switches, that seemed to go all the way down to the floor.

'Another butty, Harold?' Jammy said sweetly. Bella and I sniggered. Mam tapped me on the head and said 'sh!'

As soon as tea was over, Harold made an excuse and dashed out first. By the time we got to the door, he was heading off up the road.

'Whatever did our Harold dash off like that for?' asked his mother.

'Gone to dig up his money box, I should think,' chuckled Bella.

'I shall never understand what you have to giggle so much for, child. Come along,' said Bella's Mam, and swept away down the path, followed by Bella.

I turned to Jammy, who was his normal cheerful self.

'You won that one, Jammy,' I said. 'What are you going to do with that five bob?'

He grinned. 'Nowt. He can keep it. It was worth it just to see that look on his face. Besides,' he added and whispered in my ear, 'it wasn't a real wireless cabinet. It was an old second-hand kitchen cabinet. Dad did up and fitted our wireless into the top part.'

'But what about all those knobs?'

'Oh, he put them on for show. He uses the bottom part to keep his beer in.'

I laughed all the way home.

Any time after that, when Jammy wanted to annoy Harold all he had to say was, 'Same to you – with knobs on!'

Bella

Adam and Eve and Pinch-me-tight
Went down to the river to bathe.
Adam and Eve were drownded,
Who do you think was saved?
– Got you.

Bella was special. I thought so anyway, though I never let on. She was Harold's sister, one year younger than him and the same age as me. She had brown skin and very light blonde hair, but deep brown eyes. Her parents christened her Dorabella. They were always doing things like that. But we called her Bella.

We were in the same class at school, but girls had to sit on the other side of the room from boys, so I couldn't talk to her then. And we had separate playgrounds. We didn't meet on Sundays either, because their family went to a posher chapel than ours. Sometimes in the evening, in summer, though, when we were still in our Sunday best, the whole family would go for a walk along the Meadow. Then we'd all meet. Bella's Mam and Dad were on speaking terms with ours, though our Dad was on the Works and Bella's Dad was in business as a builder, and fancied himself a bit.

We used to pass by, hot and tight in our clothes (Bella used to have her hair pinned back till it pulled her eyebrows up) and wishing we could have an ice

cream or a drink of pop. Our Dads would raise their
hats and our Mams would say, 'Good night, then.'
Harold and I would shake our fists at one another and
Bella would screw her nose up at me.

'What are you doing?' asked her mother.

'Got a fly on my nose,' answered Bella.

'Walk straight, girl,' said her Dad.

I'd sneak a look round and put my thumb to my nose
at Harold, until I felt Dad's finger in my back.

'Stop acting the goat, lad.'

That was Sunday. It couldn't end too soon. But Saturday, that was different. On Saturday we all got together and no one watched what we were doing. Well,
not much anyway.

Sometimes on hot summer days we'd go down to the
Old River. The Old River was how it used to be, with
rapids and a sluice, where the water tumbled down
about twenty feet, foaming and boiling. The banks were
all hung over with grass and weeds. The New River
wasn't new any more. It was donkey's years since they
cut the new channel and put locks in so that the flat
boats could get up to the Works. It was deep, dirty and
dangerous and if you went on the lock gates, the keeper
might chase you off.

The Old River was deep, too, in places, but there were
sandbanks where you could wade out. It was dirty,
too, and in summer when the sun got on the water, it
stank. Our parents told us off for going there, but we
thought it was just the job.

The way down to the Old River was through the
back lanes off the main road, past a little wood, keeping well clear of the houses at Tunnel Top, because their
gang were too tough for us, and then full tilt down

Gorse Hill. Gorse Hill was steep and green with short slippery turf and dotted all over were the gorse bushes with bright yellow blossoms. When the sun went down, the hill looked as though it were on fire. Right at the bottom was an old tow path, broken here and there where the water had got in under the cinder track, and almost disappearing in bushes and weeds. We'd charge down Gorse Hill at full speed. The trick was to keep your legs going faster than your head so you didn't come a cropper – and then pull up short so you didn't run straight into the river.

We sat on the bank of the Old River one day, watching the boats pass through the locks across on the new cut. It was so hot the sweat was running down my nose, even lying still.

'Tell you what,' said Jammy, jumping up. 'Let's go in the river.'

'Don't be dopey,' said Harold. 'We haven't got our cossies.'

'I'm going in anyway,' said Jammy, peeling his shirt off.

'You're kidding.'

'Want to bet?' said Jammy, and ducked behind a bush. Next minute we heard a splash and he was in the water.

'Come on,' he yelled. 'It's smashing.' We looked round.

'Are you windy, or something?' shouted Jammy, kicking up his heels and spraying water all over the place. We didn't wait any longer. Harold and I picked a bush each and stripped down. Just then I heard a gasp from Harold. Bella was taking her frock off.

'Hey, Bella. You can't do that!'

'Get off. I want to come in as well,' she answered.

'You can't!'

'Why not?'

'Course you can't. Girls don't.'

'Ah, don't be mean, Harold. Let her come in if she wants to,' I said. 'Eh, Jammy?'

I looked round to Jammy for support, but he pretended he hadn't heard me.

'You stay on the bank and watch our clothes. We don't want kids from the locks pinching 'em,' said Harold.

So Bella stayed on the bank and looked glum while we went in the water. It was cool and smooth as milk, though the sun was hot. I jumped from a sandbank and went right down. The water was green and I could see the sunlight showing through in a great yellow patch. I burst up again in the air and got a mouthful as Harold slapped the water with his arms. I slapped back. Jammy joined in. We made such a racket we didn't hear Bella shouting at first.

'Hey, come out. It's Constable Collins.'

'You're kidding.'

'Not. He's coming up from the locks.'

We panicked. Have you ever tried to run, when you're up to your waist in water? But we had no time to stop. If PC Collins told our parents, we were in real trouble. We charged off up the bank. Have you ever tried jumping gorse bushes when you're dressed in nothing but good intentions? In ten seconds flat we were half way up the hill and hiding behind some bushes.

Bella climbed up behind us more slowly.

'Where is he?' whispered Harold.

'You keep down. Your bum's showing,' said Bella. With my head pressed down in the grass I couldn't see her face, but I could tell from her voice she was enjoying this. We lay there trying to keep out of sight and clear of the gorse bushes at the same time. I could see Jammy wriggling about.

'What're you doing?'

'Trying to get my shorts on.'

'How did you get them?'

'Picked 'em up on the run.'

'Trust you, Jammy —' A few yards away, Harold raised his voice.

'You, Bella. Where are you?'

The bushes parted. Bella flopped down by my side. Without a word, she passed me my shorts and singlet.

'Did you get our clothes?' asked Harold from the other side of the bush. She smirked, and winked at me.

'Sorry, Harold. I was in such a rush I couldn't pick them all up.'

'What am I going to do?' yelled Harold.

'Hey, shut up. PC Collins'll hear you.'

'What am I going to do?'

'You'll have to wait till he's gone, won't you? Unless you want to borrow my nicks.'

'Don't be disgusting,' snarled Harold. He glared at her and crouched down behind a gorse bush. It was painful for him in more ways than one.

Next Saturday we gave the Old River a miss. But we went down there again before the summer was out.

We had a swim now and then. And Bella came in with us. And Harold kept his mouth shut.

I'm keeping my mouth shut, too. PC Collins was nowhere near the Old River that day. Harold doesn't know that, and I'm not telling him.

Tosher

Oh, Jemima, look at your Uncle Jim,
He's in the duck pond learning how to swim.
First he does the breast stroke, then he does the dive,
How d'you like to bet me, he never comes up alive?

Tosher was a smashing lad. He was tough. When he
was only ten he had muscles on his arms like big duck
eggs, because he was always working at home. If he was
with you in the school yard all the big onks from Tunnel Top left you alone. I wanted to be his mate, but it
didn't work out till we were a bit older. Tosher was
supposed to be a bad influence.

He lived with his Dad in a cottage on some waste
ground at the back of our road. Harold's Dad reckoned
they had no right to be there. He said the place was
an eyesore. He was right, too, for the windows were
broken and stuffed up with sacking and the whitewash
was peeling from the walls. There was a black line
running along them from where their pig used to rub
itself. It was a real menace, that pig. It would run out
in the road and knock you off your bike. Then they had
hens which were all over the place. Sometimes you'd
find them hunting for food in your garden. Some people
reckoned they were a danger to traffic.

But that was a bit of a laugh. The only traffic on that
road was the Co-op bread and milk van every day and

the dust cart every Friday, and of course there was Harold's Dad's new car when they got it. But that came later on.

Tosher's Dad raised turkeys for Christmas. They were all over the road picking up a living. That was part of the trouble, because Harold's Dad had tried raising turkeys. He built a special pen for them, fed them a special diet, gave them a special tonic bought from abroad. Then they all caught a rare disease and died in early December.

No, Harold's Dad did not get on with Tosher's Dad.

Our Dad reckoned he wanted Tosher's Dad off the land so he could build on it.

'Well,' said Mam, 'that ground could be put to better use.'

'Oh, he's entitled to a place to live,' said Dad.

'It'd be better if he worked for a living.'

'Easier said than done. Eleven men after ten jobs these days.'

'Yes, and he's always Number Twelve,' said Mam.

To be fair, Tosher's Dad did have jobs now and then. He was very good with horses. He used to drive the dust cart. But he emptied the ash bins so hard the cinders flew all over the road and people started to grumble. Then he drove the Co-op van. But he got into trouble because he used to stop outside the vicarage and let the horse pee in the gutter. The Vicar's wife would come out.

'My man, must you always let your horse relieve itself outside my house?'

'Well Ma'am,' he replied. 'He likes to stand over the grid, it's more respectable.'

So most of the time, Tosher's Dad worked at home.

I used to want to go and play over at Tosher's but
Mam wouldn't let me. But we sat at the same desk in
school and shared comics under the desk. We played
a game passing an imaginary bag of gob stoppers and
chewing on them. But Miss caught us at it and made us
go and spit the toffee out. She wouldn't believe us when
we said we weren't eating anything. She thought we'd
hidden the bag and got so annoyed she made us sit at
different desks.

What with Mam stopping us playing together and
teacher stopping us from sitting together I got really
fed up with this. But one night when I was going down
to Chapel for choir practice, I met Tosher in the big
open space in the road between the blacksmith's and
Joe the Ice Cream Man's shop. Tosher had an air gun
and let me have a look at it.

'Tell you what,' he said. 'I've got a raft on our pond.'

'Get off – you haven't,' I said.

'Have 'n' all,' answered Tosher. 'Hey, are you coming
down to have a go at it?'

'Smashing,' I said. Then I remembered choir practice.
'No, I can't.'

'Ah come on,' he urged. 'I'll give you a lend of my air
gun this weekend.'

Who could say no to that? Off we ran to the duck
pond they had behind the cottage. It was dark and green
and covered with weed and hidden from the road by
thick elder bushes. It was great. First Tosher climbed
on the raft, which was made out of two old logs with
a plank nailed across, and I pulled him across the pond
on a rope. But half way over it started to sag under his
weight.

'Hey up, my bum's wet,' he yelled.

I dropped the rope for laughing and had to get down on my hands and knees to fish it out again. By the time he was on shore again, we were both wet, and green round the edges with duck weed.

Tosher felt round his back.

'Look at that,' he grinned.

All over his pants was a big green stain.

'You'll cop it,' I said.

'Never,' he answered, 'I'll rub it off and stick 'em behind the boiler tonight. They'll be dry tomorrow and Dad'll never know.'

He bent over and pulled his pants off, then his shirt, and plunged back into the pond to grab hold of the raft which had drifted off shore. 'Come on,' he yelled.

I didn't wait any longer. Shorts went one way, shirt and vest the other.

'Tell you what,' I said. 'Let's play shipwrecks – Robinson Crusoe. Here's the ship. We load up the raft. You take your gun and we paddle over to the desert island.'

We loaded up the raft with old boxes from the back of the cottage, bits of rope, a spade with a broken handle, an old hammer and a saw with a rusty blade, all sorts of odds and ends. I got ready to jump aboard.

'Wait a bit, Man Friday,' shouted Tosher, from behind the bushes.

'What are you playing at, Crusoe?' I demanded.

'We've got to have livestock,' he answered. There was a big commotion behind the bushes and a cloud of dust and feathers went up. Tosher came out clutching an old brown and white hen. She was clucking and pecking like mad. Tosher had no clothes on and she got him one or two good nips. But he only laughed.

'On board!' he commanded.

I climbed on and sat on the stores. I was a lot lighter than Tosher, but all the same, I could feel the raft sink, as the water came up round my ankles.

'Hold this,' said Tosher and shoved the old hen at me, and at the same time, he gave the raft a great push into the middle of the pond and jumped aboard.

'Full speed ahead, Friday,' he ordered.

'Aye, aye, Crusoe.'

At the same time, his full weight, on top of mine and the stores, sent the raft right under at the stern. The plank that held the logs together was wrenched off and the whole load slid off the back. I grabbed at Tosher to save myself from going backwards into the water, and let go of the hen. She pecked me on the nose, shot squawking into the air and flapped for dear life to shore.

But we other castaways never made it. Down Tosher and I went into the green and murky depths, while the logs floated this way and the stores went the other, and we splashed and shouted and laughed and choked and spat as we swallowed mouthfuls of pond water. It wasn't really deep, and we sat there on the mucky bottom, up to our chins in duck weed, while the old hen walked up and down on shore and clucked at us angrily.

Just then I noticed. The sun had gone down and the sky was growing dark. I'd forgotten the time in all the excitement.

'Hey up,' I said, struggling to the side of the pond through squelchy black mud. 'I've got to get home.'

Tosher stopped laughing as well. His Dad was due back from the Red Lion any minute now.

We dried ourselves off. Tosher used his shirt. I

thought I was smart and used my vest, so it wouldn't show.

Before I went home, Tosher handed me his air gun.

'Here. You can keep it till next week. Hey, and here's some pellets to go with it.'

When I got home I hid the air gun in the coal house and told Mam there'd been extra choir practice for the Chapel Anniversary. She was so busy she didn't pay much attention, but just said, 'Off to bed, lad.' I couldn't believe my luck as I went upstairs. I went to sleep that night thinking it was Christmas already. I could take that air gun with me when we went up the Clough that weekend. And the next week, after choir practice, I could sneak off and play Crusoe and Friday again.

But before next week comes tomorrow. When I went downstairs next day, I could see Mam had a funny look in her eye.

'You mean you went to bed like that?' she demanded.

'Like what, Mam?' I was amazed.

'Take your shirt off,' she said.

I did. Under my shirt I was green as a mermaid and my vest was like Robin Hood's waistcoat, from all that duck weed on Tosher's pond. I might have known.

Well, I got the business end of the boiler stick Mam used to stir the clothes with on wash day. And next day she stopped Tosher in the street and gave him back the air gun.

So Tosher and I didn't become mates after all. Later on we did, but that's another story.

Freddie

Please Mrs Whatsit, is Freddie coming out?
With his hands in his pocket and his shirt hanging out?

We called him Freddie the Fearless Fly and he lived in
the street around the corner from us. He was small
and so thin that a puff of wind would have blown him
away, with a pale face and a snub nose that he used
to wipe on the sleeve of one of his Dad's cut-down shirts
he always wore. It wasn't very well cut down either
because it used to stick out of his trousers at the back.

He was the eldest of about five. His father was on
the boats and always seemed to be coming or going
late at night or early in the morning. He was short
like Freddie, but broad and tough with bandy legs.
Jammy reckoned he got like this by climbing up the
masts of boats, but you could never take Jammy seri-
ously. Freddie's Dad was hardly ever home in the day
and his Mam was usually on her own – except for the
kids.

'I feel sorry for her,' said Mam, 'bringing that lot up
on her own.'

Dad shrugged. 'Maybe she's better off on her own.
You know what he's like when he's home.'

Everybody did. You could hear them in the middle
of the night, shouting. Next day, he'd be gone and she'd
be out with her pram, shopping, with a big black hat
with artificial cherries on pulled down over her eye-

brows to hide the bruises on her face. She always wore
that hat, even when she was pegging out her washing
at the back. And, when she was out, whatever the
weather she had on a tight black coat, all buttoned up.
She wore it as though it was the latest style, which it
had been – in the Great War.

Mam was sorry for her. And I was sorry for Freddie.
He used to come round and ask if I was coming out.
I used to try and be out before he came. It sounds
rotten, but you couldn't quite trust Freddie. He really
belonged with the gang round the corner. They kept
out of our street, we kept out of theirs, but anywhere
else, it was war. Anything we reckoned to do, they
reckoned to spoil.

So we kept out of their way and didn't let them
know where we were going. There were three good
places round our way. Up the Meadow where the old
oak grew. That was our place. Down the Old River by
the locks. That was risky because you had to go past
Tunnel Top. And anyway, in summer you got courting
couples in the bushes there and the men used to chase
you off. One used to carry an air gun and take a pot
at you if you got near. Then there were the woods
between the Clough and the canal. But sometimes the
gang round the corner would get there first.

This Friday evening, Jammy came round just as I was
finishing my tea. He sat on the door step so I could
talk to him through the kitchen door.

'Coming out tomorrow?'

I nodded.

'Harold's found this smashing place. He was out in
his Dad's van when they were fixing a roof out at
Millbury.'

'What sort of place?'

'There's two woods and a stream that goes from one to the other under a bridge. Hey, and farther up there's a mill and the water's really deep. There's a wheel.'

'You're not to go near any deep water.' I thought Mam had been so busy making tea she hadn't heard us.

'Oh, no, Missis,' said Jammy. 'I expect we'll stay by the bridge and we'll all wear our wellies.'

He always seemed to know how to get round people. 'I expect we'll do this,' he'd say, so no one quite knew what he was going to do. I just wasn't quick enough to think of things like that.

That night Freddie's Dad was home and there was the usual commotion, keeping two streets entertained in the small hours. Next day I was up early, chopped some firewood and got some coal in for Mam to make sure I wasn't held up for errands. I was just sitting on the back door mat getting on my wellies – a tough job because they were too small – when who should turn up in our back yard but Freddie.

His face was still smudged from where he'd been crying, his shirt tail was sticking out and he had on an old pair of tennis shoes, two sizes too big for him, and a big potato in the back of his sock.

'How are you blowing?' he asked.

'All right.'

'Are you coming out?' he said, full of hope as usual.

'Sorry, Freddie. I've got to meet Jammy and the others somewhere.'

Mam came out to the back.

'Let him come with you for once. Don't be so mingy.'

'He can't, our Mam, he hasn't got any wellies.'

'You said you weren't going near deep water.'

'Oh heck.'

'Now get on with you. Let him come, poor little jigger.'

Freddie stood in our yard looking sorry for himself.

'Oh, all right,' I said, and sloped off up our road with Freddie trailing behind. Jammy was swinging on the gate by their house. Harold and Bella were standing close by and they all looked at us and sang:

'Did you ever see a dream – walking?'

I glowered at them, and jerked my thumb over my shoulder at Freddie.

'Our Mam says I've got to have him with me.'

'Well you can flip off, then,' said Harold. 'We're not taking him. Come on Jammy, come on Bella.'

Bella didn't move. 'Either we all go or I'm stopping home.'

'Oh all right, keep your hair on,' said her brother. 'Listen you,' he said to Freddie. 'You tell anyone about this place and you get bashed.'

Freddie said nothing.

'And you follow where we lead. And if you start grizzling you can shunt off back home. We don't want any mardy cats with us.'

Freddie still said nothing.

'Oh, come on then,' said Harold and off we went, Jammy and Harold in front, Bella and I behind, Freddie trailing about five yards farther back. He knew he wasn't wanted but wasn't giving up. Nobody said very much but we all walked quickly although it was hot and I for one found my wellies getting tighter every yard of the way. We ran down the Clough and up the other side and into the fields beyond. Every so often we looked back. But Freddie was still there, padding along in his old slippers, wiping his nose every now and then.

'Shouldn't we wait for him?' asked Bella.

'Don't talk wet,' said her brother. 'Listen, when we get to Rabbit Hollow, everybody jump in quick and hide behind the bushes. He'll think we've gone on and he'll give up. Wait till I give the signal.'

Across the next field we came to a big mound where someone had started a sand pit, then given up. It was full of gorse bushes and rabbit holes.

'Now,' said Harold and we ducked in quickly. We lay still stuffing our sleeves in our mouths to keep from laughing and waited. But there was no sign of Freddie. Harold wormed his way across the grass to the edge of the pit.

'Hey up, he's gone back home. He must have.'

Jammy and I jumped up and punched each other. 'Lost him,' chuckled Jammy.

'What're you all doing down there?'

We looked up. At the top of the sand pit sat Freddie.

'Just playing hide and seek,' said Harold, sarcastically.

'That's funny,' said Freddie, 'because I could see you easy from up here.' He came sliding down the slope, rolled over and over then picked himself up and stuffed his shirt in his trousers. His face was streaked with dirt where he'd been rubbing his nose. Jammy winked at us.

'Tell you what, Freddie. You have a go at hiding, now.'

He pointed back down the track. 'There's plenty of

bushes there. We'll count hundred then come and look for you.'

Freddie grinned.

'Smashing. Bet you won't find me.'

'I bet we won't,' said Harold, jabbing Jammy with his elbow. 'Get a shift on then, Freddie.'

No sooner was Freddie out of the sand pit than Harold waved to us and charged off to the top of the pit at the other side. Inside a minute we were all heading off down the track towards the woods, looking back every now and then.

'Lost him,' said Jammy.

'Bet he's still counting,' said Harold.

Bella said nothing.

'I expect he'll just get fed up and go home,' said I, trying to make her feel better.

'Look at that,' yelled Harold, who was ahead of us. We came round a bend in the track and there in a great dip in the ground were the woods, stretching to left and right, thick and green. The path led right down into them and we could hear the rushing of water as we ran. Out of the heat of the sun, in the gloom under the trees, it was cool. An old plank bridge with a broken hand rail led across the stream which came tumbling down through the trees, foaming over stones and swirling round sunken logs. We charged down the bank and leapt in one after another. The water was ice cold, you could feel it right through your wellies. We waded out to a sandbank in the middle and crouching down, peered under the bridge where the water ran dark and deeper. A sudden splash in the still water under the timbers made us jump.

'Bet that was a roach.'

'Get off, a trout. Look at those ripples.'

Bella grabbed my arm and pointed upstream where the water cut into a sandy bank overgrown with bushes. There was a quick flash of blue. We gasped.

'A kingfisher!' Bella shouted.

'Let's explore,' said Harold.

'Which way, upstream or downstream?'

'I boller upstream. Downstream it gets too deep to wade.'

We didn't wait any longer but climbed up the bank and pushed off through the trees. It was hard going with thick briars and bushes, and here and there the ground was boggy.

'Bet no one's been here for donkey's years,' said Harold, 'this is real exploring. Glad we got rid of that drip Freddie.'

'Oh ah,' said Jammy. 'He'd only be grizzling for his Mam.'

'Ah, you've got to be tough to be an explorer,' shouted Harold and jumping into the water he led the way to the other side where the ground was clearer. We found an elder bush with long branches, cut ourselves spears and charged up and down the slopes swinging on the lower branches of the trees.

'I wonder where this stream comes from,' said Bella as we took a rest on the roots of a great beech tree in a clearing.

'Let's follow it right through,' said her brother.

'We'll have to watch the time,' said Jammy.

'Ah, come on, we've got two hours before dinner,' I said.

We pushed on. But it was a strange place. The trees

seemed to thin out ahead of us as though the wood was coming to an end, but it didn't get lighter as you'd expect. In front it was still green and dark.

'This place is getting a bit creepy,' whispered Bella.

'Get off,' said Harold, but he was putting it on a bit in front of his sister. He felt it too. The stream was narrower now and deeper in the ground. The banks on either side were higher and more slippery as though we were pushing on into a ravine. We had to clutch at branches and clods of grass to keep a hold. We stumbled and slipped and banged into one another.

Suddenly, where the wood was at its gloomiest, the stream vanished. Right in front of us like a wall rose up a great grass-covered bank, dotted with scrub. There was no way forward.

The air was colder now. The sun barely reached down here and you could see only a tiny patch of sky.

'Hey, look here,' shouted Jammy.

'Where are you?'

'Down here.' His voice sounded right from under our feet.

We clambered down through the bushes, guided by his voice and the sound of water. Under a thick, slabby clay bank, covered here and there with grass, we found Jammy, standing knee deep in the stream which was only about a yard wide but running powerfully like a mill race.

'See, it's a co'vit,' he said pointing ahead.

'What's that?' I asked.

'He means culvert, the dope,' said Harold. 'The stream comes under that whacking great bank in a tunnel, look.'

Bella and I scrambled down, holding on to each other. Deep in the bank was a dark circle of brick, dank and dripping and green with slime. We crouched down and peered in. Way in front of us, I could see a small round patch of light. The tunnel smelt foul and the air from it was freezing cold.

'How long is it?'

'Dunno. Hundred yards, maybe.'

'What's on the other side?'

'Haven't the faintest and I'm not finding out.'

'Nor me, neither.'

'Hey, what's the time?'

'Cripes, half past twelve,' said Harold. 'We'll get skinned alive.'

We struggled up to the top of the cleft where the stream vanished into the ground, slipping on the greasy clay.

'We'll never make it back, following the stream,' said Bella. 'It took us nearly two hours coming.'

'We'll have to cut straight through. Come on, get a shift on,' called Harold.

Easier said than done, though.

Walking right across that slippery slope in our wellies was no joke. The more we hurried, the more we slipped over and slid down, grabbing at grass and bushes to save ourselves. My shirt and pants were stained with mud and clay. We were for it when we got home, even if we got home in time. We ran into thicker bushes now and lost sight and sound of the stream. Ducking under branches, pushing through elder bushes, catching our hair and clothes on briars, doubling back and swerving here and there, we had no more notion of where we were going than fly in the air.

'We'd better go down and get back to the stream,' suggested Bella.

'Don't talk daft,' said her brother. 'It'll take all day.'

'It's going to take all day and night, this way,' she retorted.

At last we came on to more level ground, wet and marshy, but there was no sign of the stream. We were in an unknown part of the woods. Harold rushing on ahead went up to his knees in a bog patch and when we pulled him out he'd lost a wellington. It disappeared with a sucking sound. He said a word I'd never heard him use before.

'We'd have been better off by the stream,' said Jammy.

'Don't you start,' swore Harold. 'Anyway, we can't get back to the stream now. We don't know which way it is.'

We were lost.

'Any road,' said Jammy. 'Just as well we got rid of Freddie, he'd have been a right misery if he'd come with us.'

The ground was firmer ahead and the bushes thinner. With Harold hopping and stepping, we struggled through to a dry patch under a big beech and sat down. I suddenly realized I was worn out. My stomach was empty. I felt a bit light headed.

'What shall we do, then?' asked Jammy.

'We'll just have to go on, we can't go back,' said Harold. 'We're forced to come out somewhere.'

'I read somewhere people who are lost walk round in circles till they're exhausted,' said Bella.

'If that's all you can say, then shut your trap,' said her brother.

'Hey up.'

'Who said that?'

'Said what?'

'Someone shouted,' I said.

'Get off, you're delirious. His mind's given way,' said Jammy.

'Just shut up and listen,' I answered. To my surprise, they did. There it was again.

'Hey-up.'

'Tell you what,' I said. 'That's Freddie up there.'

'It never.'

'I tell you it is.' I cupped my hands and began to shout.

'Give over,' snapped Harold. 'We don't want him mithering round here.'

I took no notice. Any company was better than none.

'Freddie,' I yelled, 'where are you?'

'Up here, by the road.'

'You what?'

'By the road.'

The road? We stared at each other. Then we all jumped up. Freddie's voice sounded close by, to the left. Now they were all shouting Freddie's name. Good old Freddie. We followed his voice, pushed through a screen of bushes, jumped over a couple of ditches, crawled under a hedge, and there he was, sitting by the side of the road.

'Which road is this?' asked Harold.

'It's the Millbury Road,' said Freddie, looking puzzled. 'Hey, I followed you lot, when you didn't come. But I couldn't see you by the bridge, so I went right round the edge and shouted for you. I thought you were having me on, trying to lose me on purpose.'

None of us had the brass face to say anything to that. We were dead beat but we went down that road at the gallop, even Harold in his stockinged foot. We'd come out of the woods about a mile along the road from the Clough. Bella was right – we'd gone round in a big circle. We were home in half an hour and we were so glad to be there, we never minded the shouting we got.

That afternoon we met again by the old oak tree and talked over our adventure.

'Well I reckon we ought to let Freddie come with us every Saturday,' said Bella.

Harold turned his nose up, but Jammy and I said: 'Good idea.'

It was too, but it didn't work out. When I got home for tea, I saw Freddie's mother coming out of our gate. She stopped and glared at me.

'I've just been speaking to your mother.'

I said nothing, but waited.

'Our Freddie's not coming out with you lot again. I've never seen such a mess. His shirt torn, clay on his trousers, his face all mucky.'

She raised her voice so all the street could hear.

'What's the good of trying to keep your children neat and tidy if they mix with ruffians?'

She charged off and I slunk in round the back door. I took a long time wiping my feet. Mam put her head round the kitchen door. She had a smile on her face.

'Got a good telling off, did you? Well, I expect you deserved it. Come and have your tea.'

Kimmick

Oh, the cow kicked Nellie in the belly in the barn,
And the farmer said it wouldn't do her any harm,
Nelly lost her temper and kicked the old cow back,
And the farmer said he'd never thought of that.

The longest road in Tarcroft was known as the Lane.
It was like a river, starting as a cart track up by the
Meadow, where the cows grazed, then winding along
through the fields, past a farm and a little spinney
with a stream where you could play dams, if the farmer
didn't spot you. Next came the cricket pitch with an
old wooden pavilion and a flag pole. When Tarcroft
were at home, they put up a red and white flag with
TCC on it.

The Lane ran on past the 'pitch', a row of old cottages
that always seemed ready to fall down but never did,
and then it straightened out, as it passed our estate. It
was busier here with houses all along one side. Harold
and Bella lived here. Everyone in this part of the Lane
was buying their own house which was considered
very posh. On the other side of the Lane were orchards,
a sand pit and Tarcroft Athletic football ground.

When the Lane reached the middle of Tarcroft it
broadened out into an open space with a few bushes
and a seat put up for the old King's Jubilee. Beyond
that it split up into several smaller streets, like those
maps of the River Nile where it reaches the sea. And

beyond those small streets was the edge of the hill. The houses stopped here for fear of tumbling down the slope. Below there were woods full of rooks' nests in the tree tops, and big patches of stinking garlic in the spring. Half way down the hill the canal cut across, and right at the bottom ran the river, deep and dirty brown.

And on the other side of the river from Tarcroft, stretching as far as you could see, stood the Works. First the wharves where the boats tied up, then the sidings, for the Works had its own railway and engines. Then, long low sheds with their roofs crusted white with chemicals.

Beyond these were great kilns and cooling towers with chutes running down to ground level, criss-crossed with stairways and girders. Whichever way you looked on this side of Tarcroft, round the bend in the river, up stream or down, you saw the Works. If you lived close enough, you ate it as well, when the dust came through the window and peppered your bacon and eggs in the morning. Up in Tarcroft we were not bothered with that. But we could smell it – a rotten eggs smell; and we could hear it – the rattle of the chutes, the wail of the buzzer, and at night when things were quieter, the clang clang of the shunting engine bells. When the afternoon buzzer went, the men would come charging out of the gates on their bikes, over the river bridge. Some would ride along the road and up the hill. Some would dismount and push their bikes up the path through the woods. When they reached the streets at the top, they'd leap on their bikes and get off home for their warmed-up dinners.

Sometimes after school we'd go to the end of the

Lane and wait. First we'd hear the buzzer. Then, ten minutes later a great cawing and carking as the rooks stirred in the tree tops and the first men climbed up the hill. There was always something to see while you were waiting. For tucked away in these side streets at the top of the hill was another farm.

And every day, the cows used to come down off the Meadow and along the Lane, swinging their tails and splashing their muck as they ambled along, much to the annoyance of Harold's Mam and other respectable ladies.

Along with the herd came Old Bill, usually with his arm round Bluebell's neck. We used to wonder which was the older and why Bill was so fond of her. Unkind folk used to say that if he didn't put his arm round her neck, he'd fall over.

Mam said: 'Perhaps he likes the smell.'

'Get off, Mam,' I said, 'mucky old Bluebell?'

'Don't you be so sure,' she answered, 'cow's breath smells sweeter than humans'.'

'It never.'

She smiled. She knew because she worked on the farms when she was a girl.

'It does. If you ate nothing but grass, your breath'd smell sweet, too.'

'Eargh, no thanks.'

Every day, regular as clockwork, down would come the cows led by Bluebell and Old Bill. He never needed to get behind them because they followed Bluebell everywhere, and she stuck with Bill. And, when they'd passed by, there would go the Works buzzer, up would fly the rooks and the men from the Works would climb up out of the woods, on to the streets.

Often, while we were hanging about at the end of the Lane, Old Kimmick would be sitting on the King George Jubilee Bench, neatly dressed in his black·suit, shoulders well back, moustache grey and straight as a pin, blue eyes staring. They called him Kimmick, because he was always talking about the Works. 'Down at the Kimmick . . .' he would say.

He was a shift worker, but he never seemed to sleep and he was usually there when the day men came off, nodding as they rode past, like a general taking the salute.

'He's counting them,' said Dad. 'Making sure none of 'em are missing.'

Kimmick and Dad did not see eye to eye and they often argued about the Works.

'Some people,' said Dad, looking Kimmick in the eye across the street, 'would take their bed and sleep down there if they could.'

'Ah,' came the answer, 'the Kimmick's done a lot of good for this place.'

'Oh ah,' said Dad, 'and this place has done a lot for them.'

They used to argue about the war, too. Kimmick would turn out for every parade with his medals gleaming and clinking on his chest. Dad kept his in a leather case in a drawer.

I thought they couldn't stand each other, but on Works Sports Days, when they turned out for the Ambulance Brigade, I saw them chatting together like old friends. Kimmick said to me one day,

'Your Dad's like me, you know, not like these others.' He jerked his thumb over his shoulder at the houses in the Lane. 'He's seen some action.'

Kimmick liked action. When he wasn't working, or keeping an eye on the men coming up from the Works, he'd be pacing up and down looking for something to do. They always called him in when someone needed first aid. In fact they called him in when they should have called the doctor, because Kimmick cost nothing. His help and advice were free, wanted or unwanted.

We were hanging about one day at the end of the Lane and Kimmick was seated on the bench when Harold looked at his watch and said:

'What's happened to Old Bill? He's ten minutes late.'

Kimmick rose from the bench and stood near us, just as Mrs Barnes from the farm came along the road.

'Have you lads seen the cows yet?'

'No, Missis,' we all said together.

'Can't think what's happened to him,' she said. 'It's nearly milking time.'

Kimmick cleared his throat, squared his shoulders, and took command of the situation.

'You leave it to us, Mrs Barnes. We'll handle this. You lads, come with me.'

And off he marched up the Lane, like a captain at the head of his troops. I felt a bit daft as we fell in behind him and trailed along and the women looked at us over the garden gates as we passed. But Harold made the most of it saying 'yes sir' and 'no sir', to Kimmick, while Jammy thought it was a big lark. Bella said nothing but walked beside me and I think she felt it was a bit daft too.

Not Old Kimmick, though. As we passed the side streets on the estate he called out:

'Keep a sharp lookout to left and right for any signs of them.'

I didn't know about a sharp lookout. Usually when the cows passed you could see and smell it everywhere. And there were no signs of that. We stopped by the cottages while Kimmick asked an old lady.

'Good day to you, Mrs Brockett. Have you seen a herd of Jersey cows?'

She gave him a sharp glance.

'No, but I've seen Old Bill. He went up the road half an hour ago.'

'Aha.' Kimmick quickened his pace. 'At the double, lads.'

We ran past the cricket pitch, the farm, the spinney and the fields and turned sharp right to where the Lane narrowed down to a track among the trees. Kimmick stopped and held up his hand, while we all piled up and fell over each other.

'Hark!'

We harked.

Ahead we could hear the lowing of cattle. As we turned the next bend, there they were, gathered round the gate, scratching themselves on the timber and stretching their necks as they bellowed. But there was no sign of Old Bill. Kimmick turned to us.

'Two to the right, two to the left, search all along the hedges.'

We didn't have to look far. First we found his bike, lying half in and half out of the ditch, then:

'There he is,' called Jammy. Old Bill was sprawled out under our oak tree dead to the world. Kimmick bent down as if to feel his pulse and then sniffed in disgust.

'Just as I thought. Drunk on duty. Not to worry. We'll handle this.' He pointed to Harold.

'You, get the gate open.'

'Sir,' shouted Harold.

'You, you and you, follow me.' We all made a flanking movement behind the baffled herd.

'They'll give up easy,' said Jammy. 'We've got 'em surrounded.'

But it wasn't so easy. They wouldn't budge. They milled around the open gate, bellowing and pushing one another. Old Bluebell was worst of all, throwing her hind legs up in the air like a two-year-old. Back at the oak tree Old Bill woke up and staggered to his feet, shouting.

'You get your head down. You're not fit to be in charge of a bunch of cows,' commanded Kimmick. Old Bill swayed to and fro then collapsed on to the grass. But the sound of his voice started the younger cattle off. They turned and began leaping on top of one another. Soon they'd be scattered over the field.

Kimmick had a brain wave. He stepped smartly behind Old Bluebell and gave her what I thought was a vicious kick in the rear. It did the trick. With a great 'moooo' she lumbered through the gate at a trot, and the others pressed after her. The young ones tumbling behind made the whole lot speed up, jogging and swaying, lowing fit to burst with their great full udders swinging.

'Hey up, it'll be milk shakes by the time we get down there,' chuckled Jammy.

'Less of your old buck, my lad,' shouted Kimmick. 'Get in front and head 'em off.'

Easier said than done, for the Lane was too narrow to pass. Only when it widened out, past the spinney, did Jammy and I get in front and block the way. But the cattle, Bluebell in the lead, just careered past us. One jumped the verge and went through a gap into the cricket field.

'Oh heck,' said Jammy. 'If it gets on the pitch we'll be for it.'

'Head her off,' yelled Kimmick from the rear. Bella and I climbed the gate into the cricket pitch, but the cow saw us coming and doubled back behind the pavilion. When we cornered her, she crashed through the hedge again.

She scattered the others just as they were slowing down. As we reached the cottages everyone was at the gate to see us go by. I mean stampede by. I heard Mrs Brockett say : 'Well, I've never seen *Bill* bring 'em down like that.'

Her neighbour answered loudly.

'It's what they call a military operation, love.'

Old Kimmick glared at her. But he couldn't stop to argue, because the herd had reached the estate and we had to work overtime to keep them out of the side streets. The women in the Lane rushed to their gates.

'Don't you bring those cows in here, young man.'

'Keep 'em on the move,' came a roar from Kimmick.

'Sir,' answered Harold, waving a stick he'd pulled from the hedge.

But it wasn't a matter of keeping them moving but stopping them, as we very soon found out. As we streamed along across the top of our road, I heard the Works buzzer go. By the time we had reached the open space at the end of the Lane, the rooks were carking over the trees, while the cows lowed back. And the streets in front of us were all of a sudden filled with men on bikes. There was no room to get one cow through, let alone a herd.

'Head 'em off, slow 'em down,' came fresh orders from the rear. But the commander's voice was no longer heard. The cows, finding their way blocked, scattered, some into the entries and some over low walls into front gardens.

Just then from the rear came a strange, wailing sound.

'Cooooowooop! Coooowooop!'

It was Old Bill swerving down the Lane behind the route, calling to his herd. Bluebell heard his voice, stopped dead and tried to turn. But the others blocked her way. She pushed to the side, found an empty space and charged over the pavement and into the open door of the cake shop crowded with women buying tea cakes. There were screams and shouts.

An angry face appeared behind the cake stands, then vanished like magic as though its owner had been swept off her feet.

Kimmick rushed up to the shop door, shouting:

'Steady, there. We'll soon have this under control.'

But before he could get inside, Old Bill was there, throwing his bike down and elbowing him aside. For a second or two they wrestled together swearing at each other. Then Bluebell, hearing Old Bill close by, came crashing out of the shop, a cake box stuck on one of her horns, and greeted Old Bill like a long lost friend – which he was, after all.

Old Bill stood in front of the shop, his arm round Bluebell's neck, and said clearly and distinctly so that everyone could hear, 'Why don't you get back in the army. You're not fit to be in charge of a bunch of cows.'

By now the men from the Works had rounded up the cows and they were standing amazed in the centre of the open space, staring at the crowd.

Kimmick said nothing. Like an old soldier he squared his shoulders, about turned and marched away.

It was a good few weeks before we saw him sitting on the King George Bench again. And for a long time after that when the men came up from the Works, some of them would sing out as they went past:

'I'm heading for the last – round-up.'

Kimmick would say nothing but look straight ahead. A man who's seen action can face worse than that.

Miss

Glory, glory Hallelujah,
Teacher said I tried to fool her,
So she hit me with a ruler
And we all went marching home.

Miss had rosy cheeks and braided hair. The girls reckoned that if she let it down it would reach to her waist. She had brown eyes with a sad expression. Someone said she was engaged to a soldier who never came home from the War. But Jammy reckoned she was unhappy because she had to teach our lot tonic sol-fa in music lessons every week.

It was easy to upset her. Anyway our class seemed to find it easy. And the worst was if she had to punish us. I know it's supposed to be a joke when teacher says, 'This hurts me more than it hurts you.' But Miss really meant it.

The Headmistress was different. She had us all weighed up. She knew there was nothing wrong with us that she couldn't cure with a sharp rap on the bonce with her knuckles or a swift belt round the ear with a flat hand. And if that failed she'd a strap a foot long and an inch wide and a quarter of an inch thick. 'Hold your hand out,' was her favourite saying. But she was very fair. If you jerked it back, she gave you a second chance. If you jerked it back again, she'd grab your wrist and give you the first one again, then the second and a third one for luck till your hand puffed up like a rose in bloom.

But Miss, she couldn't knock a fly off a custard. She'd be afraid of hurting the fly or spoiling the custard. One time when we'd all been bad, the Head made her cane us, the whole class, starting with three each for the worst and working down to one apiece all round. Miss had a round ruler in her desk which she used for drawing lines. She didn't like it a bit, but did as she was told and went round the class, looking more miserable as she went, giving us all one or two taps and a hurt look.

We were all so ashamed we kept quiet in class for a whole week. We even tried to sing in tune in music lesson. We did everything to keep her out of trouble and us too. We knew that next time round it would be the Head and we'd be sitting on our hands for a week.

In any case whatever happened, we kept well in with Miss at the end of the week, because the last lesson on Fridays she read to us. Not *Water Babies* or *Ivanhoe*, like the Head read to us in the hall at the end of term when you had to look as if you were listening in case she asked you what she'd just said, but *Dr Doolittle*, *Swallowdale* and the latest William books. If they didn't come up with the library box every month, she'd cycle off into town and order them and pay for them herself. Friday afternoons you could hear a pin drop. She didn't mind how you sat, or if you put your head on your arm. She didn't even mind when Freddie dropped off to sleep and snored while she read. I know how he felt because when she read to us I would be miles away, one part of me listening, the other part dreaming.

Once she brought in *Winnie The Pooh* and *House at*

Pooh Corner and began to read about the time they
played 'Pooh Sticks', racing bits of wood in a stream
to see which came first under the bridge. As she read
my mind drifted away to the wood where we'd been
that Saturday, when we'd tried to lose Freddie. I could
feel the water cold round my wellies, hear the wind
in the trees, see the kingfisher flash out of the sandy
bank beneath the overhang, smell the pink campions
in the ditch under the bushes. I was so far gone I never
heard everyone else get up and head for the door. Miss
called me.

'Where were you? Playing Pooh Sticks?'

I turned red, grabbed my bag and rushed out. But she
was right. I caught up with the others in the road.

'Hey, let's go to the woods tomorrow and play Pooh
Sticks.'

'Ah, get off,' jeered Harold. 'Bags I be Christopher
Robin.'

'Give over,' said Bella, 'you enjoyed it as much as
anyone else. I saw you listening with your mouth
open.'

'Yeah, let's go up the woods,' said Jammy. 'Hey,
they'll come down a real belt just above the bridge.'

'OK,' said Harold, taking charge again. 'But keep it
dark. We don't want the whole world to know.' He
jerked his head towards the other side of the road where
Freddie was trailing along.

That night there was a storm. It woke me with the
lightning flashes through the curtain and terrific claps
of thunder. I enjoyed it, lying in bed, hearing the rain
come down. Then I remembered it might put a stopper
on our going to the woods next day. It took me some
time to go to sleep.

Morning was overcast and I had a hard job persuad-
ing Mam. But Jammy came round and said:

'It's all right, Missis, it's clear over Broughton Top.'
This was a hill about seven miles away and everybody
swore by it – better than the weather forecast, they
said. Mam looked doubtful but in the end she went out
in the garden, looked up at the sky and sniffed. When
you do as much washing as she did, other people's
as well, you know to the minute when the rain's going
to come down.

'All right,' she said, 'but don't come home wet
through, mind, I've enough to dry off as it is.'

'OK, Mam.' In five minutes we were at the top of our
road. I sneaked a look back to see if Freddie was following us. But no one was, and soon enough we were
headed for the fields with Harold and Bella.

In the end it turned out a glorious day. The clouds
broke up, the sun came through and we were soon
carrying our jackets over our shoulders.

'It's going to be good,' shouted Harold and we all
broke into a run as we came over the rise and saw the
woods. We charged down the slope like a troop of
cavalry, sending the birds up from the trees. The sun
was hot, but inside the woods it was cool and damp. If
you touched a branch overhead you were showered
with drops.

'Look at the stream,' said Jammy, 'they must have
opened the sluice.' We all piled on to the old bridge
and looked into the water as it swirled underneath. It
was dark and muddy, hiding the stones and sandbanks.

'See that current,' said Harold. He threw in a twig
he held in his hand and we saw it whirl away under
the bridge.

'Hey, how are we going to tell who wins?' he asked.

'That's easy,' answered Bella. 'Take it in turns. Three go upstream and put their sticks in and one stay on the bridge to see which comes past first.'

After some arguing over who'd be first on bridge duty we got started and the first sticks were in the water. Away they shot. One disappeared, another stuck in the side, the third went under the bridge like a speedboat.

'I won!' yelled Harold.

'You never, you ligger,' said his sister, 'that was mine.'

'Whose was it?' they shouted to me on the bridge.

But I didn't know. 'About a foot long, with two side bits,' I said helpfully.

'You're as much use as a wet week,' snapped Harold.

'Look,' said Jammy, keeping the peace. 'Let's mark the sticks. Then No. 4 drops 'em in the stream and all three wait on the bridge. Then we can all see.'

'Ah, he's not as green as he's cabbage looking,' said Bella.

Off we went again. It worked this time and Jammy won easily. Next time round it was Bella, then me. We kept scores, running up and down the bank to shout on our sticks and pushing and shoving on the bridge as they came swinging down the current to the finishing line. Just as we were in the middle of an exciting race we heard,

'Ah, look at 'em, big kids, playing boats.'

On the bank, just above the bridge, were four lads from the gang round the corner, Freddie and three bigger ones. One of them was a really nasty piece of work, called Hicksie. There was only Harold who could really fight him.

Without thinking, I shouted back.

'Don't be daft, we're playing Pooh Sticks.'

'Pooh Sticks.' They grabbed hold of each other and fell around, laughing.

'Sling your hook, you lot,' said Harold, who had no sense of humour. 'We found this place first.'

'Mess off yourselves,' came the answer, 'or we'll mess you.'

'You and whose army?'

'Just me, myself and I.'

'You couldn't fight a flea in a cake box.'

'You're windy.'

'Who's talking. Shunt off or you'll get pasted.'

Harold turned to Jammy and said in a loud voice, 'We haven't got all day. Start the next race.'

The other gang watched in silence from the other bank as Jammy ran off and threw in the sticks. I could see one or two of them, including Freddie, were getting interested. When the sticks came racing through the bridge, neck and neck, Freddie and another lad started to join in and shout.

'Tell you what,' said Hicksie at last. 'We'll race you.'

'Don't talk wet,' said Harold. 'There's no room for six boats.'

'No, one each apiece.'

Harold could never resist a challenge. I felt he was making a mistake. And I was right. For one thing it meant they got on to the bridge. For another ... But no one listened to me. They were all too excited as Harold and Hicksie ran off to cut sticks and the rest of us crowded the winning post. Harold's landed in midstream. He had more practice. Hicksie's was caught in a side current and headed for the eddy under the overhang. We started to cheer when there was a huge splash as one of Freddie's mob heaved a clod into the water.

'What are you doing?' we yelled.

'Just getting our boat free. We're entitled to do that.'

'No you're not.'

'Who's making the rules?'

Hicksie's stick, now freed from the side, shot ahead and Harold's boat, caught by the ripples, veered towards the other bank. Harold snatched up a clod and hurled it into the stream to right his own stick, but he was so mad, it landed in midstream, catching his rival's craft like a shell burst.

'You rammy git,' swore Hicksie, ripping a stone out of the exposed bank and heaving it into the water. A great spout rose and when it settled both boats were heading for the bridge.

'They're stuck together,' gasped Jammy.

'We'll unstick 'em,' said one of Freddie's mates, dodging back on to the bridge with a fistful of stones. Just as he aimed the first, I caught his sleeve. He lost balance, swung round, and his fist, stone and all, got me right in the eye. Somebody jumped on my back, Bella pulled them off, just as Harold and Hicksie, forgetting their boats, came charging on to the bridge, making the planks shake. Everyone piled in now and we rolled in one great scrum over the timbers. A side support gave way and before we knew where we were, half of us had rolled right off and into the stream, grabbing for each other to stay upright. They struggled to the side dripping wet, battered and bruised. The two boats were well downstream now and no one knew who'd won.

We trailed home, our feet sloshing in our wellies and our shirts steaming in the sun. We were all in for it; a good start, but a bad end to Saturday.

On Monday, when we went into school, Miss took one look at me and gasped.

'What have you done with yourself? Where did you get that black eye?'

'Playing Pooh Sticks, Miss,' I answered.

She looked at me and said nothing. But I don't think she believed a word I said after that.

Boakie

Boakie Boko is no good
Chop him up for firewood
When he's dead, boil his head,
Make him into currant bread.

Tunnel Top was a place you left alone. You couldn't reach anywhere by going down there anyway. The road curved down the side of the hill and ended where the canal ran underground for a good half mile. But that wasn't the reason for staying away. Down Tunnel Top lived the families who worked the narrow boats on the canal and the flats or dumb barges on the river. They were rough and the people up the hill looked down on them. But some of their families, men and women, had worked the barges for two hundred years, and their motto was – if you don't like us, leave us alone.

With Boakie it was different. He didn't like you, but he wouldn't leave you. Thumping was his favourite game and he played it well. You gave him plenty of room. The trouble was even if you could fight him, he had a brother in the big school who was built like a brick wall. And they had more brothers and cousins and mates. They ruled Tunnel Top and the ground over the tunnel. This was a valley with steep sides and great towers with open tops to give air to the boats as they went by underneath.

At one time, they used to unhitch the horses at Tunnel Top and lead them over to the other side, while the boats were pushed through by hand and foot against the tunnel wall. Then they brought in a little tug with a two-stroke engine which would draw a string of barges through the tunnel. If you sat on the bank on the farther side, you could hear the chunk chunk of the motor inside the earth. The tug would sweep out of the narrow mouth of the tunnel and swing round in a wide arc. The tugman leaned out so far on his tiller you'd expect him to fall into the water. Then he'd cut the engine and the narrow boats came gliding out.

They slid along like wagons on a train, each one casting off the tow ropes and steering clear of the one in front until they came to rest at different points along the tow path and the lads brought the horses down from the top to hitch up. You were all right at that end of the tunnel but if you walked over the top and down the valley where the airshafts were, you were in Tunnel Top territory and you had to look out for yourself. Tunnel Top kids kept clear of our streets except when they came to school. If Boakie had his way, he'd never have come there at all. That was his one trouble in life. He might be boss in the school yard, but once inside the school door, he was done for. He was afraid of only one person in life, apart from his Dad, and that was the Headmistress.

She came no higher than his shoulder. He could have picked her up and carried her out as easy as wink. If only he'd dared. But he didn't. Poor old Boakie. I used to feel sorry for him when she had him out in front of the class, which was once or twice a week, when he'd forgotten something, couldn't say his times table, or spelt a word wrong. One day he was writing an exercise in pencil and made a mistake. He had no india-rubber, so he felt inside his jumper and pulled out his vest with round rubber buttons on. Bending over his book, nose on the desk, he tried to scrub out the word he'd written wrongly. Inside five seconds the whole line was a grubby brown mess. What was worse, while he crouched over his book, the Head stood by his desk and watched. The rest of us, rotten lot, sniggered and waited to see what would happen next.

She took him by the ear and lifted him up. She might be small but she was strong. He was dragged out in front of the class and made to stand there. He could go and sit down as soon as he told everyone what he'd been doing and remembered how to spell the word which was now smeared all over his exercise book.

The class was quiet.

We waited. But not a word came from Boakie. For one thing he'd no more notion how to spell the word, than fly in the air. For another he wasn't going to give us the big laugh he knew would go up as soon as he admitted what he'd done.

So he stood and sweated, drops forming at the end of his nose, his face creased up like a boxer's, his eyes blank. Not a word came out. Every two minutes, the Head would say, 'We're waiting.'

But Boakie couldn't or wouldn't speak. His face grew more crumpled and miserable, the sweat drops rolled down his chin.

'Hey,' whispered Jammy, 'he's going to start skriking.'

But Boakie didn't skrike. He found a loose stitch in his jumper, gritted his teeth and began to work his hand round and round.

'We're waiting,' said the Head.

Round and round went the hand, while Boakie stared at a corner of the ceiling and the sweat rolled down inside his collar. Soon the hole was wide enough for two fingers.

'We're waiting.'

We held our breath. But not a sound made Boakie. His whole hand was inside the gap in his jumper, winding round and round.

'We're waiting.'

Now the whole front of the jumper had given way and the strands were wrapped round Boakie's fingers. The bell went for dinner. We all let our breath go at once. The Head marched out of the room. We stared. Was she letting him off? But at the door she turned.

'What your father will say about your jumper I can't imagine.'

Boakie's red face went grey. Someone started to laugh. It spread. Jammy nudged me. He looked straight in front of him, his face like an owl. I did the same. Jammy was no fool.

Miss came back in to the classroom and dismissed us. We piled into the school yard. As we rushed out, I could hear a yowl from someone and the familiar sound of thumping.

Then came Boakie's voice.

'You were laughing, weren't you?'

'No, I wasn't, Boakie, honest.'

'Ligging little git. You were grinning all over your fizzog.'

We sneaked away to the school gate. We didn't stay to watch. This morning Boakie had copped it from the Head. Tonight he'd cop it from his Dad. But just now, he was handing it out.

Boakie has his Day

You may not believe this, but the day came when we all stood up and cheered Boakie. 'Good old Boakie,' we shouted, that day. It happened at Tarcroft Fete.

We were always glad when the Fete came round. The fine weather seemed to arrive to stay on that weekend. You knew that summer was here and before long there'd be the big holiday. Skies were blue, the smoke clouds over the Works seemed lighter, though there was nothing you could do about that rotten eggs smell. Hay was drying in the fields, the bogs in the woods were golden with king cups and the dog roses were out in the hedges.

First thing in the morning Tarcroft Silver Band in their red and blue uniforms were on the streets having a run through of the tunes for the parade, *Colonel Bogey* and *Blaze Away*. Old Bill was always in form, because he was the drummer and you could hear him beating time from one end of Tarcroft to another. He was so good they reckoned that one time he took a wrong turning and marched down one road while the band marched down the other, yet when they joined up again at the corner, everyone was still in perfect time.

The Morris Dancers and Sword Dancers and Maypole Dancers came from miles around to compete, the Rose Queen was dressed up in her finery and best of all, we thought, the Fair came around again and parked on the

Football Ground, next to the Meadow. When the Fete ended in the afternoon you could go from one field to another just for the one threepenny ticket. If you went home for your tea, the man at the gate would stamp your wrist with a date stamp, so you could get into the Fair again in the evening. And if you had a mate who hadn't a ticket, you pressed your wrists together so the ink from the stamp showed on their skin as well. Of course the date was the wrong way round, but the gate men never noticed, or if they did, they never said anything.

But the real excitement of the day came in the annual contest with Fairham, a village about three miles away, long our sworn enemies.

There'd be races, wrestling, team events with people entering from all the places around. We weren't interested so much in who won, but whether we beat Fairham or not. It was all unofficial but we kept a strict score. Last year they'd beaten us in the annual cricket game, a real needle match, that. So by the time the Fete came round again we were ready for revenge.

At first it looked good for Tarcroft. Our ambulance men beat theirs in a display of stretcher work, how many broken legs you could splint up and cart off in three minutes.

When our team beat theirs in the relay, it was in the bag, we thought; though we were a bit too quick, because the show was only half over.

One after another, they won the greasy pole, the sandbag match and the egg and spoon race. But the real blow came with the dancing. Their team carried it off with some very fancy work, while ours was nowhere.

Towards the end of the day we were just level pegging and the excitement was tremendous. The Fairham
lads started to pelt us with orange peel and screwed-up
programmes. We might have hit back with something
more solid. But the stewards came round and threatened
to belt us all if we didn't stop. But even they couldn't
stop the riot when the judges announced the Fairham
St George and the Dragon had won the fancy dress
parade while our Robin Hood and his Merry Men had
only come third. There was a lot of muttering about a
fixed match. They began to chant.

'Tarcroft, Tarcroft, nowt in the hayloft.'

Which meant we had no brains. Cheek.

We answered back with:

'Fairham, Fairham, where they canna spare 'em!'

Which meant, as everyone knew, that they were
tight with their money over there.

But they had the edge on us and the afternoon was
nearly over. We could shout all we liked, but if they
held on to their lead, they'd be laughing.

Last in the day came the big jazz band parade with
teams from all round playing penny whistles and
kazoos, marching and counter marching. The women
worked for weeks beforehand making the uniforms and
the bands practised every day making a terrible din.
It was the best thing in the whole Fete and we always
cheered them on and off the field. But this time the
mood wasn't so cheerful, especially when we saw the
Fairham mob march on with scarlet jackets and gold
braid, blazing away like one o'clock.

'I reckon they must have a tame millionaire fitting
them out with those jackets,' said Jammy. 'It's not
fair.'

On came some more bands, one after the other, marching and playing well, but not a patch on the Fairham lot. Our hearts were in our boots when the announcer shouted through his megaphone:

'Make way for the Tunnel Top Jazz Band.'

On they came, twenty strong, big and tough looking in sky blue and silver shirts, white pants, and fantastic big peaked caps that looked a foot tall, and big horns fitted on the kazoos to make them look and sound like trumpets. They played *Blaze Away* as they stepped in, all in line and all in tune.

'Hey, look who's there,' said Harold, nudging me.

I stared. Look who was there.

Right at the front with a great stick with silver tassels jerking it up and down to the sound of the music, was Boakie. As they swung past our part of the field, giving the eyes right to the judges, Boakie slung his stick ten feet in the air and caught it again and twiddled it like a plane propeller.

There wasn't a doubt. We all knew even before Tunnel Top marched off. They were best, we were best. Tarcroft had leathered Fairham and that was the end of that. The cheers went up as they marched off.

'Tarcroft to win. Good old Boakie.'

Patch

Patch was my dog. Well, he was in a way. When the family next door moved out, a widow woman came to live there. The gossip was she used to run a pub and was a bit fed up with always having people round her. So she never went out but sat in her front room in her best dark velvet dress all day with her two dogs stretched out on the carpet. One dog was like the old lady. He never went farther than the back door and then only when desperate.

But Patch, her second dog, liked people and liked to be out of doors. So I took him for walks. Or rather he took me. He was a kind of cross between an Airedale and a Labrador, brown as a fox (in fact a farmer nearly shot him once) with a patch over one eye. If I went out in the yard and whistled, he'd shoot out of next door on to the pavement and then leap our front gate, stopping in mid-jump, all four paws balanced on the pointed gate posts, before jumping down. I was always scared he'd trip, but he never did.

He'd go anywhere with you, charge after a stick, leap a hedge or ditch, swim a stream. When we ran in the woods on the hill above the Works, where the garlic plants grew by thousands in spring time, he'd roll in them down the slope and come up smelling like a pizza. Or he'd jump in the canal to get at his own reflection and come up smelling like nothing on earth.

His eyes were big and brown and he was so full of

good will it's a wonder his tail stayed on his body. If you had a wrestle on the grass, he'd join in, though sometimes he got over-enthusiastic and bit everyone. It was lucky he did it gently, Mam said, or he'd have your leg off. We were in no danger, though, because Patch never bit anyone in anger in his life (except once). To tell you the truth I began to think he was a bit too easy going, a bit of a coward in fact.

One day, when we were out walking, as we passed a farm a great black dog charged out of the yard, barking furiously. Patch immediately moved over and put me between himself and the black one. Not only that, he suddenly started limping and looking sorry for himself. We drove off the black dog with a few well-aimed sticks while I examined Patch. As it happened he had a thorn in one of his pads, so he wasn't putting on an act. But I felt he hadn't really matched up to my expectations. He was big enough to look after himself, I reckoned.

The truth was, of course, that he didn't like fighting. If he was in the road and saw the whacking great white-grey Alsatian who belonged to Hicksie, round the corner, Patch would slip over to the other pavement and look for a hole in the hedge.

He preferred small dogs, and when Jammy got a puppy, Patch was delighted. It was about as mixed as he was, a kind of spaniel cum dachshund, very low on the ground with floppy ears and appealing eyes. They took to each other as soon as they met and always stuck together when we were out in the country, though Flip, Jammy's dog, hated water as much as Patch loved it. But it was a treat to watch them rolling about together when we came to a clover field or going mad

72

racing in circles and barking when we went to Rabbit Hollow. They were real mates.

In the middle of Tarcroft there was this open space, in front of the Co-op, with the ice-cream shop on the corner, where Joe sold ice cream in summer and fish and chips in winter. When he drove his van round the streets you could hear his handbell ringing and everyone came running. On the other side of the square was a blacksmith's and when the farmers brought their horses in to be shod, we used to gather round to see the sparks fly and the water boil when the hot iron was plunged in. Everybody came there at some time or other, and it was a kind of Tom Tiddler's Ground: nobody ever started a fight there. We used to leave each other alone. The trouble was, dogs didn't know this.

One Saturday morning we were hanging about waiting for Joe's to open, when I noticed Patch behaving in a funny manner, walking round my legs, twisting his lead round my arm, as if he were trying to hide. I looked round. Sure enough, there was Freddie's mob from round the corner, about six of them, standing by the blacksmith's. The big Alsatian was wandering about loose, scratching the ground and making horrible snuffling noises.

Just then his tail went up, he sniffed the air and came trotting over to us. Flip, no more than a puppy still, and innocent with it, pulled loose from Jammy's grip and went up to sniff at the big dog. It was the worst thing he could have done, for the next moment he was rolled over on his back as the Alsatian went for him.

'Hey, call your stupid dog off,' yelled Jammy. He was as scared as Flip. But across the square they only laughed while their dog got on with eating Jammy's.

But right then I felt a tremendous jerk on my wrist – it almost pulled my hand off. Then another wrench. The loop of the leash came off and like a brown streak, Patch went for the Alsatian. There was a snapping and a snarling, a rolling and a cloud of dust, and a yowl from one of them, I couldn't see which, because now one of them was on top and now the other.

Then the bigger dog was running for his life, tail between his legs. From across the square came an agonized shout.

'Hey, he's bitten a lump out of his nose. That dog of yours ought to be shot.'

'Your dog ought to pick somebody his own size,' yelled Jammy, who was holding Flip in his arms and trying to pat Patch at the same time. I couldn't help it. I burst out laughing. Bella and Harold joined in.

I called across the square. 'My dog's going in for an ice cream. When he comes out, he's going to eat yours for afters.'

When we came out of Joe's with our ice-cream cornets, the square was empty.

Ollie

One question we used to argue the toss about when we were sitting in the oak tree on the Meadow, was – Is Blind Ollie blind or not?

'He must be,' said Bella. 'He goes around with a white stick. You can hear him tapping miles away.'

'Oh ah,' said I, 'he's like Blind Pew in *Treasure Island*.'

'Well, I reckon he's not blind,' said Harold. He was in his contradicting mood.

'How do you make that out?' asked Jammy.

'Well,' said Harold. 'He always knows if you're following him.'

That was true. It was a game we used to play. Everybody did it. We'd line up behind Ollie and walk along in single file. The first one behind him had to see if they could touch him on the back. You had to be quick as greased lightning or he'd turn round like a flash and give you one with his stick, and that hurt.

Of course we stopped that game. Miss gave us all a real telling off in school one day.

'I will not have you tormenting Mr Hargreaves,' she said. 'It's wicked.'

We sat there open-mouthed. What was she talking about?

'How would you all like to be blind, like him?' she asked. I could see she was really mad and I felt bad.

'She means Blind Ollie,' said Tosher in a stage whisper.

'I mean Mr Hargreaves,' rapped Miss. 'And if I hear of any of you playing that nasty following game again, I'll ...'

We held our breath. Was she threatening to belt us?

'I'll send you to the Head.'

That was enough. From that day on, no one followed Blind Ollie as he tapped his way across the square by the Co-op. The funny thing was I noticed him one day, peering round now and then as he walked, muttering, 'You wait, I'll paste you if I catch you.'

I remembered this when we were sitting in the tree.

'What do you reckon he was on about?' I asked the others.

'Maybe he thought you were following him?'

'But I wasn't anywhere near him.'

'Blind people have very good hearing,' said Bella.

'Well, I still reckon he's not blind,' repeated Harold, 'and I'll tell you for why.'

We waited.

'You know when they chopped that old oak down, next to Tosher's?'

We nodded. We'd all gone down the Lane to see it. The huge old tree, nearly as big as a house, had been badly felled and crashed down across the Lane, blocking it.

'Well,' Harold went on, 'do you remember when they were breaking it up to cart it away, they put wedges in it, didn't they?'

'Oh ah,' we three all said at once. We all remembered the iron wedges giving off sparks as the sledge hammers struck home.

'And, who finished it off?' demanded Harold.

'How do you mean?' I asked.

'It was Ollie, wasn't it?'

It was. In a flash I remembered Ollie shedding his old coat and rolling up his sleeves. I saw his bare brown arms, thick and knotted like an oak branch, swell as he spat on his hands and took up the sledge. Then, crash, crash, crash, three blows, one on each wedge, and the trunk sprang apart and the pieces fell to either side.

'He never missed, did he?' asked Harold triumphantly.

We were silent. There was no answer to that. We had all watched it and the funny thing was, I'd thought nothing of it at the time. When people do something very well you don't notice them doing it, it seems so natural. But Ollie was supposed to be blind.

'So there,' Harold added. 'How could he hit those wedges if he was blind?'

'Perhaps he was used to doing it before he went blind?' put in Bella.

'My Dad says Ollie's always been like it,' answered Jammy. We sat a while and weighed that up.

'Let's do an experiment,' said Harold suddenly.

'Experiment?'

'That's it. Try it out with a hammer and some wood.'

'Hey, we've got some firewood at home and I can borrow one of Dad's chisels,' said Jammy. His Dad didn't seem to mind him messing about with his tools.

In ten seconds we'd all piled out of the tree and were racing off down the Lane to Jammy's place. His mother looked a bit suspicious when we all suddenly arrived in their back yard offering to chop wood.

'What do you want a chisel for, our Alan?'

'Oh, the old axe is all blunt,' said Jammy, quick as lightning.

'Well, take it all down by the shed. And mind what you're doing.'

'Oh, it's all right. I can chop wood with my eyes shut,' said Jammy. We all burst out laughing and Jammy's mother stared.

'You mind what you're doing, d'you hear?'

We all rushed off to the back of the shed and had a quick scrum over who was having first go. Harold was first. He took up the hammer, closed his eyes and made a big swipe. But he not only missed the chisel which Jammy had tapped into the wood block. He missed the block altogether.

Jammy had a go, missed the chisel, but hit the block and split a chunk from it. Now it was my turn. I rolled up my sleeves and spat on my hands like I'd seen Ollie do.

'Give over,' said Harold, 'your name's Simpson, not Samson.'

'Shut up,' I answered, 'I'm concentrating.' I shut my eyes and swung.

The hammer hit my toe and I hopped about in agony. The others hooted which didn't do my toe any good.

Then Bella had a go. She took the hammer and laid it to the wedge.

'Hey, that's cheating,' said her brother.

She ignored him, drew the hammer up in a careful line and then brought it down squarely on the chisel.

'You had your eyes open.'

'No she didn't,' Jammy and I spoke together.

'Give's a go,' shouted Harold, mad as he always was when his sister got the better of him. He swung the hammer up, eyes closed, until it rose well above his shoulder, ready to bring his clenched fists violently down. But his hands were sweaty with the heat. The hammer slipped, flew backwards over his shoulder and went clean through the shed window.

In two seconds flat, Jammy's mother was on the spot.

'And who said they could chop wood with their eyes shut?' she demanded.

We couldn't help it. We all burst out laughing again, which only made her even more mad with us. She only calmed down when Harold ran off home for some money and got a pane of glass from the paint shop. By the time Jammy's Dad came home, the window was mended.

But the argument about Ollie's eyesight was never settled. After all, it's not something you can ask someone, is it?

Jack O' Lantern

This night we come a soul-caking
Good night to you,
And we hope you will remember
That it's soul-caking time,
Folly-dee, folly-di, folly-diddle-i-o-day
Up with your kettles and down with your drums
Give us an answer and we'll be gone
Apple, pear, plum or cherry
Anything to make us merry.

Autumn was here and the dark evenings drawing in. Along the Lane, where the gas lamps stopped, it was black as pitch and the wind made eerie sounds in the trees. It was near the end of October and soul-caking time had come. In some places they call it Hallowe'en. Nothing so fancy for us. We called it soul-caking time because we went round singing for pennies. People had mostly stopped giving you little cakes or fruit, but we didn't mind because we were saving the pennies for Bonfire Night.

So we went round and sang:

'And the next day it is Lord Nelson's, a hero is he,
With a bunch of blue ribbons tied down to his knee,
And the medals on his breast like stars they do shine,
And we hope you'll remember that it's soul-caking
                                                    time.'

This verse used to annoy Miss, I think, because Trafalgar Day was 5 October, and here we were at the end of the month. But we couldn't help it if it wasn't historically right – that was what the song said.

Besides, it wasn't history we had on our minds this soul-caking season. It was revenge. Our gang had had a bad year at the hands of the mob round the corner.

It started on April Fool's Day. Nothing wrong in that, of course, just a lot of daft tricks. When someone rode by on their bike you'd shout, 'Hey, your back wheel's going round,' and hope he'd get off and look, and so on.

They'd tricked us by sending Freddie round with a message that they were giving away apples up at the farm and we'd all trooped up there, to find out it was just a gag. By the time that was done it was too late to think of a trick to get our own back.

Then on Oak Apple Day at the end of May, you were supposed to wear a sprig of oak leaves in your button hole, or you were scutched on your legs with a bunch of nettles. They ambushed us on our way up to the Meadow to the old oak tree. Our legs burned like mad till we found some dock leaves to rub on.

After noon on Oak Apple Day, comes Legging Over Time, when it's everyone for themselves. The idea was to trip people up by fair means or foul. The favourite trick was crouching down behind someone, while your mate caught his attention. Then a third lad ran up and gave him a good push so he went head over heels across your back. The other gang caught us at the bottom of our road, when they outnumbered us. They even got Harold down. Then they did a bunk and we couldn't catch them.

By autumn time we already had two grudges to work

off and we were ready for desperate measures.

'I've got an idea,' said Jammy.

'Oh ah,' we said, doubtfully.

'The gang round the corner are going soul-caking on Friday.'

'Queen Anne's dead as well,' said Bella.

Jammy ignored the sarcasm.

'It'll be dark up the Lane when they finish doing the cottages.'

'Ah?' We paid a little more attention, now.

'So we hide in the hedge and jump out as they come past?' put in Harold.

'Get off,' said Jammy, 'we put the wind up 'em.'

'How?'

'With a turnip head.'

'Not bad.'

But Jammy wasn't finished yet.

'You know Millbury Dun?'

We stared. Of course we knew Millbury Dun. Who didn't? It was a famous race horse which died years ago and was buried in the park up at the Hall. Old people reckoned that on stormy nights it rose from the grave and galloped along the hedge tops.

'Right. Our Gran's got an old rocking horse she's going to throw out. The rockers are all broke and the stuffing's coming out.'

'So?'

'So, we get the head off it. We get a white sheet and we dress up, two of us, as Millbury Dun.'

'Oh ah,' I said, 'and we jump out at 'em from behind the hedge.'

'That's him. But first we stick the Jack o' Lantern up on a stick and poke it over the hedge. I mean, I do that. Then Bella gives a scream and neighs like a horse. She's good at that.'

'Ta very much,' said Bella.

'Then you and Harold, dressed up, charge down and stand in the way. They'll have forty fits.'

'I'm not sure I want to be a horse,' said Harold. 'I'd rather stick up the turnip head.'

Jammy shook his head. 'Boller me Jack o' Lantern. It's my idea.'

That settled that. We got to work quickly, for we only had a day or two. Jammy made the turnip head, scraping out a really big turnip and cutting eyes, nose, and a jagged line of teeth in the side. I had a good idea too. I borrowed my brother's bike lamp to put inside, much better than a candle. Bella persuaded her mother to lend her an old sheet for some 'play acting', only she didn't tell her Mam what sort of play acting it was. So by Friday night we were ready to go.

Just after sunset we were hiding behind the hedge that runs between the Lane and the cricket pitch. We heard the mob from round the corner go by; they were aiming to sing at the farm houses.

There you still got apples and pears given you and a drink of dandelion and burdock.

We could hear them singing farther up the Lane. It was so dark you could hardly see the houses just a little way down where the first street lamps reached. The wind got up at dusk and you could hear it moaning in the tree tops across the field.

The singing came nearer – if you could call it singing.

'*This night we come a soul-caking, Good night to you.*'

'Hey,' whispered Bella, who was keeping watch

higher up. 'They're at Bowyers', that's the last one. Get ready.'

After a bit of arguing the toss and pushing and shoving, Harold and I got dressed up. He wore the horse's head and I crouched behind him, wrapping the sheet round us. We shuffled over to a gap in the hedge. There was an easy way over the ditch where someone had filled it in with timber. About ten yards along, Jammy switched on the bike lamp inside the turnip. It suddenly grinned out green and horrible in the dusk.

'Hey up, keep it down,' mumbled Harold inside the horse's head.

'Don't be daft. They can't see it through the hedge.'

Bella whistled. Up the Lane we heard:

'*And we hope you'll rem. mber that it's soul-caking time.*'

'You'll remember all right, mate,' muttered Jammy. I started to giggle and fidget.

'Give over,' snorted Harold, 'you're tickling my bum.'

That only made me laugh all the more till Harold kicked back with his heel and caught me on the shin. I gave him a sharp dig with my knee.

'You mingy –' he grunted, and swung round digging his elbow in my face. I side stepped and the horse began to come apart.

'Stop your messing, you two onks.' Bella was right next to us now. 'They're coming.'

Right then we heard footsteps in the Lane.

'Now,' whispered Bella.

Right on cue, Jammy hoisted up his stick with the turnip top so that it grinned over the hedge.

From the Lane came a gasp and a muffled scream.

'Come on,' spluttered Harold, trying to set his horse's

head straight, as we charged off through the gap in the hedge. From our right came a shrill neighing sound from Bella. Harold and I crashed through the gap a little out of line, because the head was skew-wiff on Harold's bonce. We missed the timber pile and went head-first into the ditch, grabbing at each other to try and break the fall.

'Wheeeeee,' whinnied Bella.

'Whooooooo,' Jammy joined in.

'Give us a hand up, you daft 'aporth,' gasped Harold.

By the time we were out of the ditch and free of the Millbury Dun outfit, the road was empty.

'Wish we'd seen 'em run.'

'They had the wind up all right. Hear that screeching?' said Jammy.

'Come on,' commanded Harold. 'Let's get after 'em with the turnip head. We might catch 'em.'

'Just a minute.' Jammy had bent down and was peering at the ground.

'What're you doing, you wet Nellie?'

Jammy pulled the bike lamp out of the turnip.

'Look at that.'

We stared. As large as life, lying on the ground, was a big ball of knitting wool.

'Hey up, it's moving.'

So it was. As we watched the ball jerked forward and began to roll down the Lane in front of us, with Jammy in hot pursuit, while we leaned on one another helpless with laughter.

'They must have had their mother's knitting,' he shouted between laughs. Twenty yards along he caught up with the ball, picked it up and began to reel it in as he capered along the road.

'Diddums drop his mammy's knitting then?' Diddums get a fright from the nasty ghost?'

Still shaking and laughing he vanished in the dark. We followed on more slowly but still chuckling, Harold with his horse's head tucked under his arm, me with the sheet round my shoulders.

There were sudden footsteps in the Lane. Round the bend in the hedge appeared the turnip head, bobbing and jerking, but still with its ghastly grin. Jammy was running, but in the opposite direction, and behind him were two figures. Voices were raised in the dark, there was no mistaking whose they were.

'Just wait till I catch him, our Betty, I'll give him turnip top. I'll tan his backside.'

'Cripes,' said Harold. 'It's Mrs Bowyer and her sister. We picked the wrong people!'

Still holding up his turnip top, Jammy galloped past us, swerved to the right, cleared the ditch and went headlong through the hedge. Without stopping to think we followed, rolling down in the grass on the other side.

'Switch the lamp off, you daft object,' gasped Bella. The ghastly grin vanished from the turnip's face.

'Now run for it,' hissed Harold.

'No, wait,' whispered Bella.

On the other side of the hedge there was a tremendous commotion. The Bowyer sisters were shouting at the top of their voices.

'You think it's clever do you? Come round soul-caking one minute, then scaring the life out of people the next.'

'But, Missis,' we heard Hicksie's indignant voice.

'Don't you contradict me, young-feller-me-lad. Just

wait till I tell your father. He'll tan your backside for you.'

'But we weren't doing anything. We were just walking down the Lane.'

'Well if it wasn't you, then who was it?'

'I don't know,' said Hicksie, 'but I can have a good guess.'

Harold nudged me. Silently we gathered all our bits and pieces and stole away into the night.

King Arthur

I'll never forget that weekend, for two reasons. For one, Dad brought me home a second-hand bike. It was like Jammy's, it had belonged to someone smaller; but Dad adjusted the saddle so I could ride it without my knees hitting my chin when I pedalled. I was no longer odd one out as I had been since Bella got a bike for her birthday.

For another, that was the weekend Jammy and I met King Arthur. That was unforgettable. At least Harold and Bella didn't let us forget it for a long, long time.

On the Friday night we'd come out of school early and were up on the Meadow when Old Bill fetched the cows down. He'd forgiven us by now for the time we'd helped bring the cows home and nearly wrecked the centre of Tarcroft. Besides, he liked someone to talk to and he was full of stories, real old ones, like the tale about the big round cheese that rolled over hill and dale letting all the poor folk take one bite and singing, 'I'm for the needy not for the greedy'; or the Asray who lived at the bottom of Millbury mere and vanished when a fisherman caught her and tried to take her home; or the headless calf that used to run along the lanes on dark nights. I was glad it was daylight when Bill told that one, and I tried not to think about it when I went to bed that night.

But the best story was about the farmer who lived

up in Broughton Hills and owned a white horse. When he became poor and had to sell it, he was met on the way to market by an old man who offered him ten times the price for it. He was so curious that he followed the buyer, who led the horse away into the hills and then vanished into a cave. There in the depths of the hill was a huge stable with twenty stalls. In nineteen of them were white horses fast asleep. The horse he had sold was led into the twentieth stall and there it instantly fell fast asleep.

Beyond the stable was a great hall with a huge round table. By it sat twenty knights in full armour, fast asleep. But the old man turned and caught the farmer following him. So he made him swear secrecy and promise to tell only his own son on his death bed. In the cave, said the old man, were King Arthur and his knights, waiting to be woken if the country was in danger. But they could not sleep easy until a twentieth horse was found. With that the old man sent the farmer away, the rocks closed behind him and the farmer could never find the way back inside the cave, no matter how he searched.

This story took Old Bill all the way down the Lane and we stood there after he'd gone, thinking about it.

'Do you reckon it's true?' asked Bella.

'Well, King Arthur existed,' I answered.

'Ah, it's just a story,' said Harold, which was right enough.

We set off slowly for home.

'Tell you what.' Jammy stopped. 'Dad reckons there are caves in Broughton Hills that have never been properly explored. They go right inside the mountain.'

'And you reckon King Arthur's sleeping there?' jeered Harold.

Jammy shrugged.

'It'd make a right old racket,' went on Harold.

'What would?'

'Twenty horses and twenty knights snoring, and all that armour rattling.'

'You've no soul,' said his sister.

There was no more to be said. We all went home.

I hadn't been there more than half an hour when Dad came with the bike. I couldn't wait to try it out. I'd had a go on Jammy's old cronk often enough. Inside minutes I was in the saddle, down our road, tearing round the next road and into the Lane. Just as I took the corner, at about sixty, a cat ran out from the pavement. I took a short cut right into the hedge.

I picked myself up, straightened the wheel, looked round to make sure no one had seen me and then rode straight down to Harold and Bella's house. The Lane slopes down there so as I came to their gate, I was going a fair old lick. Just then I saw Bella in the front garden and took one hand off the handlebars to wave to her.

'Now then, Bella-a-a-a-'

My wheel hit the kerb, the bike and I left the road and hit their front gate. Luckily it was open and I shot through and sprawled all over the garden path. I heard Bella's mother screech.

'Harold. Tell that boy not to ride on our flower beds.'

'Hey, look who's dropped in,' said Harold as he came running out of the side entry. He looked at my bike spread all over the path, and bits of the path spread over me.

'We had one and the wheel came off. Where did you pick up that old cronk? Been round the rubbish dump?'

I raised the bike and straightened the wheel again. Then I stared Harold down.

'When you've done, I was going to suggest a bike ride tomorrow,' I said loftily.

'Where to – the infirmary?'

'No, to Broughton Hills.'

'Get off with your bother. I'm not towing you back.'

'Please yourself,' I answered. 'Jammy and me'll go. We'll take sandwiches and pop and look in the caves. Want to come, Bella?' I said craftily.

She nodded.

'See you tomorrow, eh? About nine o'clock.'

Harold waved his hand contemptuously. 'I'll stay home and listen to the traffic bulletin.' He put on a BBC voice. 'Pieces of an old rusty bike are holding up traffic between Broughton Hills and Tarcroft.'

I ignored him, waved to Bella and rode off. This time I stayed in the saddle.

After a quick call at Jammy's, I spent the evening practising left and right turns, giving signals, braking, mounting and dismounting. I only came off twice.

Next day we took the road for Broughton. Harold was with us, of course. We had sandwiches and bottles of pop in our saddle bags. It was only seven miles away but we reckoned to make a day of it. Jammy and I were determined to go through every inch of those caves. It was hard work getting there, one slope after another, and we had to get off and push every now and then. But it was smashing when we arrived, hills covered with bracken and gorse stretching all round and an old ruined castle right at the top. Harold made us climb the slope and have a look round the castle, some old broken down walls and a well with an iron grating round it. They reckoned there was treasure at the bottom, but it was three hundred feet down.

'Bit of a swizz really,' said Jammy, 'twopence each to look at a lot of old stones. Come on, let's get down to the caves.'

'OK,' I called and charged off down the hill.

'I'm not looking at any rammy old caves till I've had my baggin,' said Harold grumpily. And for once, Bella sided with her brother. 'I'm puffed out. Let's have our sandwiches first.'

By the time we'd eaten and rested a while, Jammy and I were getting really impatient.

'Come on, you two. To the caves. Charge,' we yelled. They followed us slowly and came to the caves just after we'd arrived.

It was dead cold after the sunshine and once we were away from the entrance it was dark, and sticky-slippery underneath. Water from the roof dripped down our necks.

'Hey up,' said Jammy, 'we should have brought a torch. You can't see a thing in here.'

'You can smell plenty,' sniffed Bella. 'What a pong. Like ten trillion cats.'

'Get off,' said her sarky brother. 'That's not cats. Somebody's been mucking out King Arthur's stables.'

'Ah, belt up,' said Jammy, 'you spoil everything.'

'Any road,' I said, disappointed. 'This one doesn't go any farther.' We turned back and trudged out to the entrance. Now the sun struck warm on our arms and faces.

'Just look at my tennis shoes,' said Bella in disgust. 'There were ten trillion dogs in there as well.'

'Come on, Bella, I'll help you clean it up,' said Harold.

Jammy and I stared at each other. 'Wonders'll never cease,' Jammy muttered. Harold and Bella sat down on the grass and began to clean up her tennis shoes. Jammy and I waited and fidgeted.

'Come on, you two. There's five more caves to explore,' called Jammy.

'Oh, you carry on,' came the answer.

'Ah, come on, Jammy,' I said. 'Let's go in ourselves.' He nodded and we plunged into the second cave entrance.

'Wouldn't it be smashing if we found something really old – like a spear or a sword.'

'Ah, wouldn't it just.'

But the second cave was just as dark and smelly and empty as the first and so was number three. The fourth one was narrower and longer and as we tramped in, Jammy's foot struck something which gave off a metallic sound. Eagerly we scrabbled it up from the cave floor and hurried out into the sunlight.

'It's curved and hollow, a bit like a gun barrel.' Jammy sounded as excited as I felt. But once outside he hurled it down in fury.

'A flipping old handlebar.'

'Found something?' shouted Harold.

'You wait and see,' I answered and we ran back into the next cave, which was lighter and drier.

'I can smell something strange here.'

'I know what it is. It's wood ash. Somebody's made a fire. Wish we had a torch. D'you suppose there could still be cave dwellers in here?'

'Shouldn't think so. It'd be in all the papers.'

'Ah, but suppose they kept in here and only came out at night. Like the Clay Men in *Flash Gordon* or something, and we were the first to find them.'

'Hey up, then, maybe they won't want us coming in here. They might be desperate.'

Jammy raised his voice. It sounded a bit funny, like I felt.

'Don't be afraid. We mean you no harm.'

His words echoed a bit in the cave roof and there was a sliding noise as something dropped down. We turned and ran, falling over each other. At the cave mouth we stopped. Behind us there was dead silence in the darkness.

'Perhaps there was nothing there after all.'

'Anyway, let's go and have a quick look in the last one. We can always come back when we've got a torch.' I wondered if Jammy could tell my voice was shaking a bit.

'Do you think we'd better leave the last one alone?'

'If Harold sees we leave one out, we'll never live it down.'

'Well, then, let's go a little way in.'

'OK.'

The last cave was bigger, and about twenty yards in it split into two branch tunnels.

'Shall we each take one?' Jammy was whispering now.

'No, let's stick together,' I whispered back.

The passage was narrow and we had to go in single file. It curved and the light vanished behind us. I trod so close behind Jammy that when he suddenly stopped I banged into him.

'Hey, what're you playing at?'

'L-look,' he said.

I peered over his shoulder. Ahead of us the passage

widened out and some ten yards away, from near the cave roof, shone a flickering light. We crept forward, clutching one another. The light came from a sort of lantern stuck on a ledge in the wall. By its gleam we could see vague shapes, one like the edge of a table and a chair.

'Look.' Jammy's voice had almost vanished in his throat, as he pointed down.

There was straw scattered thickly on the ground. We froze. From only a few feet away, it seemed, came the sound of deep, regular breathing. Someone was fast asleep. Thoughts flew across my mind – tables, chairs, straw, stables, someone sleeping.

'Jammy,' my voice was a squeak. 'Do you think we've found that secret cave?'

He didn't answer but pointed a little to my right, just underneath the lantern. There, stretched out, half visible in the dim light, was the figure of an old man. His face was in shadow but a ray from the lamp showed the beard that flowed down over his chest. As we looked he stirred in his sleep and turned. The light fell on a thin timber shaft that lay in the straw at his side. It was like a spear.

We backed slowly away until we were out of the side passage. Then we turned and ran out into the light, shouting, 'Harold, Bella.'

Reluctantly they got up from the grass and came towards us, while we rushed down, slipping and sliding. We both spoke at once.

'A stable, straw, a table, a lantern, an old man asleep ... and it looks like he's got a spear.'

Bella's eyes grew big and round.

'Get off,' jeered Harold. 'You're making it up.'

95

'Come and see then.'

That shut him up. They followed as we climbed back to the cave mouth and in down the smaller passage. For a moment I thought it might all have vanished. But no, there was the light on the wall. I heard Bella gasp.

There wasn't much room as we all crowded into the passage. As we reached the wider part beyond and heard the sound of breathing once more we were pressed up so close together someone's foot caught my ankle. I tripped and staggered forward, falling across the sleeping figure.

There was a strangled roar as it came to life. The others fled with me close after them. As I stumbled down the narrow way I heard footsteps behind me and an angry voice. Into the main passage we tumbled, pushing and shoving at one another to get into the open air. As we reached the light the voice behind us became clearer.

'You gormless young articles. I'll knock your blocks off if I get my hands on you.'

We turned.

In the middle of the cave mouth, rubbing his eyes with one hand and shaking the other fist at us, was a tramp in an old tattered overcoat. His long, grey hair hung down in rats' tails round his red, weatherbeaten face.

'Didn't mean to wake you up, Mister,' shouted Jammy nervously.

This only enraged the old chap. Stooping, he began to claw up stones and clods from the cave mouth and hurled them at us. We didn't wait any longer but rushed down the hill, not stopping till we reached the place where we'd stowed our bikes under the hedge.

The old man came half way down the hill, still flinging clods and curses as he went. But by now we were on our bikes and piling down the road.

Just before a turn in the road took us out of sight, Harold lifted in his saddle, turned and shouted as loud as he could, 'Beg pardon your Majesty,' then rode on, choking over his own joke. Bella began to laugh, too, but Jammy and I rode on in grim silence.

We knew we'd not be allowed to forget King Arthur for a long time.

Ollie's Story

I found out more about Ollie quite by chance. It happened like this. My Mam made smashing cakes. Her treacle parkin, dark and rich, was a big favourite, but her malt loaf was famous. I liked everything she cooked or baked, but I'll let you into a secret. There was something I liked better, though I would never admit it to her.

I couldn't stand Mondays. The wash-house was full of steam all day, the fire going under the boiler, the dolly peg pounding up and down in the tub. There was the smell of soapy water as Mam fished up great swathes of washing with the boiler stick and fed them into the mangle, while the wheel went grinding round and the bluey water streamed over the rollers. It all started about six in the morning and it was still going on when I got home from school. If it rained on Mondays then the whole kitchen would be lined, floor to ceiling, with washing, and I'd grumble that you couldn't see the fire. Mam would shrug and smile and give me sixpence to go round to the cake shop. For sixpence you got sixpenn'orth of stales — fancy cakes left over from the weekend: cream horns, iced slices, jam puffs. There was something special about those stales on Monday. If they were dry I never noticed. It was the cream, the icing, the layers of jam, the red and green decorations. And since I got them from the shop I had first pick before my brothers and sisters.

Tuesday was ironing day with a friendly warm smell from piles of smooth white sheets and pillow cases. Wednesday night the washing would go in a basket and I'd walk up the Lane with Mam after dark to deliver it. Once I asked her what she did when she couldn't sleep and she said, with a smile, 'Count washing.'

But, I was talking about cakes, wasn't I? Mam's malt cake was so tasty, with a crust on it that melted in the mouth, that everybody wanted the recipe, which she kept written out on a small slip of paper. She lent it out now and then for others to copy as a favour – not that they could make it like she could.

One summer evening I was sent down with the recipe to the locks on the river. The lock-keeper's wife was to have it. Straight down and straight back was the word and I honestly meant to do just that. The trouble was they had a big garden and orchard at the locks with ropes to swing on from the trees and the locks family was big and friendly. When I finally got away and started to run up the hill, making up my excuses as I ran, the sun was setting down river and the sky beyond the canal bank above me was changing from light to dark blue.

I ran with my head down, not looking where I was going, and almost had my foot on the stile that led to the tow path, when I stopped short. The way was blocked by a broad back in an old striped shirt. Above that a thick, brown neck and straggling grey hair. And beside the figure on the other side of the stile was propped a battered white stick with the paint peeling from it. My heart came into my throat. It was Ollie, sitting right bang in the middle of the stile. I was so scared of him I didn't dare ask him to move. Who knew what he'd say, or do? But if I didn't get home, there'd be more trouble. There was a gap, about big enough for a dog to get through, under the stile, just by Ollie's feet, in their huge, scratched, hob-nailed boots. Quick as a flash I dived down, wriggled under and scrabbled to my feet on the stones of the tow path. But, as I came upright and made to sprint off down the tow path, my arm was seized in a grip so hard I gasped with pain. Fear made me angry.

'Hey up. You're hurting.'

Ollie turned his brown face with its roughened skin and I looked into his eyes for the first time, large, up-turned, white, criss-crossed with bright red veins. They swivelled so far up under the pink-rimmed eyelids that the pale-blue irises seemed to vanish.

'Shut thy gob and sit down.' His voice was quiet but he wasn't letting go.

I sat down unwillingly on the bottom rung of the stile, his huge leg touching my shoulder. He released my arm, but I felt he would know the instant I stirred. In front of us the canal was as smooth as glass, catching the purple of the sky. Beyond, the thick bushes stood out black. Everywhere was still.

'Hark,' he said.

From the thicket over the canal a bird began to sing. I'd never heard it before, but I knew what it was as the first notes flowed out in the evening air. It was a night-ingale. I held my breath, while the bird sang on and the sky darkened behind the bushes until they were one black mass.

The song ceased. Ollie stood up.

'Hast'a heard that before?'

'No.' My voice was small.

'Say nowt and hear more, look t'ee.' Ollie picked up his stick. Made bold by his sudden friendliness, on impulse, I passed my hand in front of his eyes.

'What dost'a think tha's doing?'

'Nothing.'

I wanted to hurry away, but he put his hand on my shoulder from behind and we walked along slowly. I found my voice. 'Mister –' I couldn't remember his name. 'Mister – Ollie, if I don't get on whom, I'll get shouted at.'

'Eh? We'll go Tunnel Top way. That's quicker.'

Tunnel Top? My stomach chilled. We had come to the tunnel where the path forked. I wanted badly to sneak off to the left, but the hand on my shoulder pressed me forward.

'Tha Dad works at the Kimmick,' said Ollie.

'Ah.'

'Got his foot burnt in the caustic, didn't he.'

'Hey, that's right.'

'Bad old place, the Kimmick. My granddad was a waller – digging salt in the old days.'

We were deep into the valley over the tunnel now, with the setting sun behind us, catching the top of the ventilation towers.

'All round here's built on salt,' Ollie went on. 'And you know what they did? They dug great mines underground and left big pillars of rock salt to hold up the roof.'

'Was that round here?' I asked in disbelief.

'No more than two miles away, up the canal,' he answered. 'They had one mine so big there was a dinner down there, with lights and all, and the King of Russia came. What dost'a reckon to that?'

'What, underground?'

In the dark before us I could see the whitewashed cottages of Tunnel Top and, dimly, the waters of the canal beyond. People were standing and sitting at the doors staring at us as we came down, me in front with Ollie's huge hand on my shoulder.

'Ah, underground. All eating and drinking. And none of 'em thought what they were doing. All they thought on was getting the salt out and selling it. Then one day, the brook flooded.'

'Hey, which one was that?'

'The one that runs under the canal, through the co'vit. It got into the workings. All the salt went into the water. Down came the pillars and down came the ground on top. There was a hole three hundred foot deep.

'It made great flashes in the ground and the houses around all sank, till there was no village left, just a cinder track between the lakes.'

Just then I noticed from the corner of my eye a crowd of people outside one cottage. I knew it was Boakie and his family, staring at Ollie and me and not saying a word. Ollie must have known they were there. He half turned and said:

'Good night then,' and I added quickly, 'Good night.'

'Good night then,' they answered, still staring.

We came to the main road. Ollie went on with his story.

'Even houses in the town sank down in the street. One month they were street level, next they had to have steps leading down to 'em. In the end, they'd to build shops on frames so they could jack 'em up. The old salt firms reckoned it wasn't their fault, said it was an Act of God. Well, God wasn't digging that salt out. So in the end they had to pay up, something any road.'

'Hey, Ollie, is that place still like it? All lakes — flashes and sunken houses?'

'Oh ah. There's some good fishing in those flashes.' He turned to me in disgust. 'But, you know what the Kimmick's doing? Filling 'em up with waste, with rammy green muck — Ah!'

We were at the bottom of our road now. I could see the women at the gates under the street lamps. Mam was outside our front, arms folded, talking to the neighbours across the street. She saw me.

'Wherever have you been? You should have been back hours ago.'

Ollie spoke up.

'It's all right, Missis. He's been seeing me home. Good night then.'

And he was tapping away up the road.

I was bursting to tell Mam everything, but she just said:

'Get along in. It's long past your bed time.'

But it was a long time before I could get to sleep. The night was warm and the window was open. I could hear the women talking below and in the distance down the hill the clang, clang of the shunting engines running through the Works. Lying in bed I thought about the flashes and the old salt workings and the houses that sank into the ground and all the unbelievable places Ollie said were just two miles up the canal.

Freddie has his Day

One, two, three
My mother caught a flea
She put it in the teapot to make a cup of tea
The flea jumped out, mother gave a shout,
In came Dad with his shirt hanging out.

One Saturday night – no, it was Sunday morning because
I heard the church clock strike twice in the distance –
I woke up with a jump. I'd heard a noise in my sleep.
For a second or two I lay still in the dark, trying to
make up my mind if it was a dream or not. Then I
heard it again, just a little way away – round the corner
in the next street. An angry yell, a scream, a bump and
crash, then silence. Freddie's Dad was home off the
boats. In the darkness I could hear Mam and Dad talking in low voices.

'Don't know why she puts up with it.'

'What can she do? Anyway, she makes out it's not
happening.'

'She told me the other day, he's not a bad bloke
really. Looks after them, always brings home something
for the kids.'

'You wouldn't think so to look at Freddie and the
others, poor little jiggers.'

The voices died away. There were no more bumps
and bangs in the night and I drifted off to sleep. On
Monday, Freddie was in to school as usual, his nose

running, his elbow out of his sleeve, spuds in the heels of his socks, slouching along in his oversize tennis shoes with the toes out. And his mother was out doing her shopping in her long black coat and the big brimmed hat pulled down over her eyes.

I felt sorry for Freddie. Everybody pushed him around. Even his own mates just had him as an errand boy. And our gang didn't want him. When he called round to our house now and then, Mam would look at me as much as to say 'be decent'. That would just make me feel more awkward and unfriendly to him. But, hearing all that carry on in the night suddenly made me feel sorry. I nodded to him across the road.

'Now then, Freddie. How're you blowing?'

But, you know, he didn't even answer. He walked on scuffing his toes in the ground. I thought to myself – all right, stitch your own britches, then, and left him to it.

That day Freddie got into a fight. The first in history. He fought his own way, too. He kicked. That didn't do much harm because his toe was about half a mile inside his tennis shoe. But he scratched as well. His opponent got a beauty right down his nose that put him out of action. We didn't know what to make of it. He hadn't scrapped fair. That was bad. But he'd won. That was good. And the other lad was bigger than him. Everybody was. He was getting on for eleven, but he looked as if he'd just come out of the infants. They still all left him alone now, but it wasn't for quite the same reason. 'I mean,' said Jammy, 'scratching like a cat, or a dog.'

A couple of days later, on the Wednesday or Thursday it must have been, there was a big commotion at school. Freddie had done something, answered back to

Miss, used a dirty word, so one of the girls reckoned. He was sent to the Headmistress, who didn't waste any words, dirty or otherwise on him, but gave him the strap, six on each hand. At least she started. But at number four he gave a yell, snatched the strap out of her hand, flung it across the room, knocking a plant pot off the window ledge, and ran off home.

More ructions. Freddie's mother was sent for, and when I was coming out of the cloakroom to go home, a bit after the others, I saw Freddie's mother standing in the corridor talking to the Head and using that posh voice which always made Mam smile.

'I don't protest to contradict you, but my son does not use such words. I can tell you that if we heard any such thing, my husband would have his belt off to him. We're very strict on things like that.'

And with that she stalked out, managing to keep her back straight and her head down and face hidden with her hat brim as usual. But Freddie didn't come to school next day.

His mother asked me to take a note in to Miss.

'I bet he's not ill,' said Jammy. 'I bet he can't sit down.'

'More likely can't stand up,' said Harold. But nobody was laughing. I had this feeling there was more trouble brewing, like a storm building up before you get thunder and lightning.

We didn't have to wait long. That very night, just after I'd gone to bed, it started again, in the next street. It was as clear as if it were in our garden, bumps and bangs, a scream, then I heard Freddie's voice, shouting.

'Wait till I get my shoes on.'

All of a sudden there was a bigger crash, then silence

for a few minutes, then footsteps running down the street in the darkness, then silence again. I could hear Mam and Dad talking in the kitchen downstairs. Then they began to come up to the bedroom.

'What do you reckon's happened?'

'We'll find out soon enough tomorrow. You know what it's like round here.'

And we did. On Saturday afternoon, when the men came up from the Works, I saw Dad in the street with his bike, talking to Kimmick. Dad was speaking quietly, but Old Kimmick just didn't know how to. He always thought he was on the parade ground.

'Got called out last night,' he was saying.

'Oh ah?'

'Round the corner.'

'Ah.'

'Case of concussion and delayed shock.'

'That's bad. Is she all right now?'

Kimmick grinned.

'Not her – him. Out like a light. She told me he tripped and hit his head on a chair.'

Kimmick paused.

'Tell that to the marines. Somebody was holding that chair when it hit him.'

Kimmick paused again.

'About time too.'

'Who did it?'

Kimmick shrugged.

'Your guess is as good as mine. I've got my suspicions, though. Cheerio, then.'

He marched off down the road. Dad saw me listening and frowned.

'You keep all that to yourself, mind.'

I did too, though it didn't make much odds, for every street round about was talking about Freddie's Dad and his 'accident' with the chair.

But there was more to come. On Sunday evening, we were all dressed up and walking over the Meadow, after Chapel. I heard Dad say,

'Wonders'll never cease.'

And Mam answered,

'Sh, she'll know we're talking about her.'

Along the path towards us came Freddie and his Mam. She had his hand tucked under her elbow as they walked. We all stared. We couldn't help it. She was in a new coat with a new hat like a pill box perched on her head. She was made up, too. And Freddie – he was in a grey suit, long 'uns and all with a red handkerchief in his top pocket.

As they came level, they both turned to us.

'Good night then.'

'Good night then,' we answered.

We walked on without saying anything for a while, then Mam said:

'Freddie looked well in his new suit.'

'Ah,' said Dad, 'quite grown up.'

The Co'vit

I was in my last year at our school when I had a row with my mates. A real fall out. I didn't see them for weeks. We hadn't been out a lot together just then because there was so much homework. The scholarship exam was coming up in the summer and that was the big thing. Only about fifteen from our school had ever got into the grammar and their names were written up in gold letters on a board in the hall. You'd think it was the Olympics, only without the fun.

So we had our heads down and didn't see all that much of each other. We were drifting away a bit. But I suppose there was more to it than that. In fact, I know there was. It was really my fault in a way. I was wanting to share a secret with my friends and keep it to myself at the same time. It's impossible, but there you are.

We fell out one Saturday over where we wanted to go. I wanted to go to Millbury Woods. Harold and Jammy wanted to go to the Hall.

'You can't get up to the Hall, any road,' I said grumpily. 'The gamekeepers'll stop you. Tommy Mills got shot up there.'

'That's what he says. He's a rotten ligger,' said Harold.

'Hey,' said Jammy. 'Come on. It's smashing up at the Hall once you get in over the wall.'

'Yeah, I know,' I jeered, 'miles and miles of wet rhodondendrons.' But I spoiled the sneer because I couldn't say the word, let alone spell it.

'Nah,' Jammy grinned. 'I heard Dad say there's a lot of statues there, women with nothing on and that. You don't find that in Millbury Woods.'

'There's better,' I said.

'Well, what?'

'Well, lots. There's the bridge, and the stream and boat racing.'

'Ah, that's ancient ...'

I wanted to say — there's the co'vit. But I couldn't make myself utter the word. After all those things Ollie had told me I just wanted to keep it to myself. If I told the real truth I really didn't want them with me. Yet at the same time, I was a bit scared of being on my own.

So when Harold and Jammy said they wouldn't go to the woods, I was half pleased and half annoyed. I looked at Bella hoping she'd decide to come with me. But she didn't. She didn't even say :

'Aw, come on with us.'

In which case I might have changed my mind.

But she said nothing.

'All right,' said Harold, 'be on your own, you misery,' and they turned their backs and walked off up the road.

So in the end I set off for the woods in a bad mood. I was annoyed with them. And I was a bit annoyed with myself. The weather was hot and close. There hadn't been any rain for a fortnight and the fields were yellowing in the sun. The turf on top of Rabbit Hollow was brown, and heat haze was rising on the skyline. My wellies were tight on my feet and the sweat ran down my neck. By the time I got into the woods I had a headache and I was parched. I lay down on the bank above the bridge and had a drink from the stream. It tasted bitter and strange.

Under the trees the air was still and stuffy. Every move in the grass and bushes brought up a cloud of insects that settled on my face. Time and again as I trudged on upstream I wiped them off or flapped my hands to get rid of midges and gnats which hung in clouds over the water. The going became rougher as the ground sloped upwards. I noticed too that the woods were darker than usual. The sky, when I caught a glimpse of it through the trees, was a strange, darkish, steely colour, as though a big lid had been pulled across and the woods, with me inside, were shut under it. There was no sound, no birds, no small animals rushing off in the bushes.

It was strange. It was as if the woods and the sky were waiting for something and I began to turn round to see if I were really alone.

Now I was in the high part of the woods, scrambling on the slippery overhang with the stream in its narrow bed beneath. The light grew dimmer, the great bank of the canal loomed up in front and the sky overhead had changed from steel grey to steel blue. The sun had vanished. I stopped to get my breath, hooking my arm over an overhanging branch. The culvert I knew was just ahead beyond a fold in the ground.

With a deep breath and a count of twenty I let go of my branch and half ran, half slipped over the rise in front of me and came right up against the huge wall of earth and grass that towered up above, holding the canal. Twenty yards to my right was the culvert, a black oval in the green. I sat down and slithered sideways over the sloping turf until I could steady myself on the moss-covered brick arch of the tunnel entrance.

A breath of damp, stagnant air came up and I shivered. Below me the stream coursed out of the ground, its waters foaming and gurgling over the brickwork. I could not tell how deep it was here. There was nothing for it but to go down. Digging my fingers into the brickwork set in the bank I lowered myself carefully down the six-foot drop to the bottom curve of the tunnel. Just as I tried to shift my hold to a crack in the lower brickwork, my foot slipped. Down I went, jarring shoulders and hip, landing on all fours in the water. I felt it flood into my wellies as I grabbed for the tunnel edge and hauled myself on to the brick curve above water level. The sides were green with slime and hard to hold on to. Three times I slid back before I got a proper grip and stood, clinging to the inner wall.

Ahead of me the tunnel stretched dark and cold, but at the end was a faint oval of light, like the far mouth of the canal at Tunnel Top.

But this was larger and nearer. I reckoned it was fifty yards to the other side. I put a foot out along the brickwork, slipped and found myself sliding into the water again, but clutched in time at a split in the brickwork. My hands were coated with slime now, but I held on. I had no choice. I could not move forward without slipping. Nor could I move back without letting go. Behind, the woods were in thick gloom; ahead, the tunnel even darker.

As I hung on there, the sky over the bank split in a silver vein of forked lightning and a massive thunder clap shook the bank. I thought my ear drums would meet in the middle of my head. Without thinking I clapped hands to my ears, let go of the brickwork and went sliding down the greasy circle of the wall into the water. At the last moment I saved myself by throwing my body across the channel so that my hands struck flat against the opposite wall. I was clear of the water but stretched out across it like a mad diver, not falling down but not able to get upright again.

Outside, more lightning. The thunder rang down the tunnel till I thought the whole bank, canal and all, would give way and bury me. I remembered all Ollie had said about the land caving in and my inside went cold. I tried to push up with my hands but the strength was gone from my arms. Yet I couldn't stay there. I knew that. I told myself, saying it out loud. But I could not push upright. Arms and legs were numb with strain, stomach chilled with fright.

The rain was flooding down outside now and as I looked at the stream rushing down the channel below me, I noticed something that made my heart give a jump. The water was turning brown. I knew right away what that meant. The water beyond the canal was rising, the mud stirred up in the stream bed. Before long it would come through the narrow hole in a torrent.

The thought gave me strength. I jerked both hands from the wall and tried to come upright again. But fell back. This time, though, my hands had shifted a foot along the brickwork. To keep my body straight, I edged my feet sideways, farther into the tunnel.

It struck me right away. This was the way to go. Sideways. I jerked up my hands again and half-fell to the right, breaking my fall again, hands on wall. Then I shifted my feet again and again. I was moving like a crab about a yard a minute, but I was moving. Forgetting the thunder, the lightning, the flood water, my fears, everything, I set my mind on getting through that tunnel. At the end of the culvert the white circle grew lighter and lighter. I made out the stream on the other side, high green banks and overhanging willow trees. Beyond that a slope with more trees. I speeded up, slipping and sliding now and then, but more sure of my feet and hands, until with three last sideways heaves I was on a ledge at the lip of the tunnel on the other side. I was through and at the edge of the little green valley with the stream now foaming with flood water in front of me.

Overhead the thunder died away, the rain stopped and above the trees the dark sky opened into blue, grey and white streaks. As I jumped from the ledge to the bank of the stream to clamber to the top, the sun came through, suddenly warm on the back of my neck. At the top of the valley I paused and looked back. Behind me the great canal embankment and the tree tops beyond. But ahead!

I stood and stared. From my vantage point I could see a whole new world, great patches of water glinting in the sun, islands with purple flowering bushes, huge weed-covered cinder heaps, ravines filled with shrubs, a winding track and broken white bridge, and beyond, roofs and walls half sunk into the water. This was the place Old Ollie had told me about, where the land had given way and the water rushed in. I felt like every explorer since time began. With a yell I rushed down the track towards the bridge. Half way there I stopped and turned aside to peer down into a gully, full from top to bottom with blackberry bushes, a mass of blossom. Wait till I told our Mam. We'd pick tons of berries here in August and September.

Running on I caught with the corner of my eye the shine of sun on glass. To my left was a ruined house, like a farm.

Leading up to it was a splendid row of white- and pink-blossomed horse chestnut trees. There'd be millions of conkers in a few months' time.

I followed the track where it ran, banked up with ash and cinders between the flashes. Now it wound up to a ridge and as I mounted this I saw I was only on the edge of my discovery. Before me was a great stretch of bush-studded moor, with larger lakes, clumps of small trees and, like an ancient city, the ruins of old workings, a network of grass and moss-covered walls forming caverns and arches, trenches and dugouts. I dodged madly among the ruins, peering here, poking there, noting in my mind places to explore when I had more time.

Beyond the workings, more open space with more blackberry bushes than I'd ever seen in my life. Farther off still, more flashes glinting in the hot sun. At first I did not grasp it, but these flashes did not reflect the sky. They had their own colour, a weird emerald green and whitey blue. It was not water, but a great expanse of chemical waste stretching in front of me, dead like some landscape on the Moon. I pulled a brick from a broken wall and hurled it into the nearest pool. It rested a second on the green crust and then sank slowly into the ooze.

I looked around me now, for I'd been running and charging round for about an hour. The woods and canal were well behind me. I was alone in my own fantastic world. But where was I?

Then I saw on the skyline, the unmistakable great

grey-brown plume of smoke that marked the Works. I
headed towards it and beyond the last green-blue lake,
came to a final ridge and looked down into the valley,
at the curve of the river and farther along the wooded
hill that marked home. Half an hour later I'd reached
the canal a mile or so from Tarcroft and was trotting
along the tow path. I ran easily as if my excitement had
given me second wind. The damp in my clothes had
dried in the sun. As I ran, the Works buzzer sounded
across the river.

I stopped, alarmed. Was that the 12 o'clock or the
one o'clock?

Down the slope I saw the men on foot and on bike,
stream over the bridge. They were heading away from
the Works. It was 12 o'clock. It was amazing. All the
things I'd done and I'd only been away three hours and
I could get home easily for dinner. It was just right,
smashing, a bonzer day and all on my own.

After dinner I rushed out in the street. I wasn't going
to call for Jammy or Harold or Bella, oh no. But if they
happened to be around ... I might just tell them a bit of
what they'd missed. But there was no sign of them. They
must have gone off somewhere. I felt flat after the
morning's excitement.

I trailed off along the Lane, half hoping they might
be there, but the Lane was empty. I wandered round
corners and side turnings until I heard shouting in the
distance. There was a football game on the rec. Might
as well go and watch. It wasn't a real game, just a crowd
of kids booting a ball between the goal posts, charging
about in a big crowd, changing position. Even the goalie
was up with the rest, trying to score.

The ball shot out of the scrimmage and landed near

my feet. I belted it back and a lad trapped it with his foot. He grinned and waved. It was Tosher.

'Hey up. Come on. You can be on our side.'

I didn't waste any more time but rushed in kicking with the rest.

'Haven't seen you down here in donkey's years,' said Tosher.

'Been doing things. Hey up, Tosher, there's a smashing place down the canal ...'

The Lewis Gun

Will you come to Abyssinia, will you come?
With your ammunition and your gun?
Mussolini will be there, shooting bullets in the air,
Will you come to Abyssinia, will you come?

When Mussolini, who was dictator in Italy, started on little Abyssinia, there were big arguments in the school yard. The newspapers had pictures of Abyssinian troops firing old rifles and grass huts burning, when Musso's planes bombed them. Everybody reckoned it ought to be stopped.

'My Dad reckons Musso and Hitler can be stopped if all the other countries gang up on 'em – look, there's Britain and France and Holland . . .' I said, counting off on my fingers. Everybody agreed. My Dad had been in the Great War and in the artillery, too. That meant he knew about fighting. So there it was.

At home, in an old biscuit tin there were dozens of postcards with coloured pictures of India, Greece, Belgium, France, showing strange towns and encampments, soldiers crouching behind guns, or sitting in trenches smoking and seeing in their dreams a misty view of a cottage with roses round the door. I used to look at these cards on rainy days and think about the war and soldiers and wonder if all the things in the newspaper, about Hitler and Musso, meant there'd be another war. I asked Mam and Dad about it, but more often than not they changed the subject.

But it seemed to come nearer. Hitler kept on invading other countries and no one seemed able to stop him. Then the newspapers and the wireless began to talk about Czechoslovakia. No one could say it, let alone spell it, but we heard the word more often than we heard Tarcroft. It was over there in Europe and Hitler was moving in. Now there might be a war.

One Saturday I went down to the rec to play football with Tosher and the other lads. Mam didn't know and I didn't say anything. She didn't know Tosher like I did.

This time, when I ran in through the rec gate, I pulled up short. Our football pitch, or rather the grass patch we'd worn bald with playing, was roped off. Some council men were digging a hole in the ground, watched by Kimmick, Old Bill and some other men. I saw Tosher hanging about. He looked excited.

'Hey up. They reckon there's going to be a machine gun here, for if Hitler invades.'

'Get off.'

He drew his hand across his throat.

'No kid.'

We pushed up to the ropes. A fair old crowd had gathered now and Kimmick was holding forth.

'It'll be a Maxim or a Vickers, that's for sure.'

'Never,' said Old Bill, 'a Lewis Gun.'

'A Lewis Gun,' snorted Kimmick. 'You can't stop ought with a Lewis, it's not got the weight, and it jams as soon as you touch it, and . . .' he paused to make sure his audience was listening, 'it lacks the accuracy.'

Old Bill ought to have been flattened.

'All right then,' he said calmly, 'where's your emplacement, your sandbags?'

'There's your emplacement,' said Kimmick, pointing at the hole in the ground.

'Get away with your bother, you couldn't put a man and a flop gun in that. That's to mount a Lewis Gun.'

'And I'm telling you, it'll be a Vickers at the very least.'

'Want to bet?' said Old Bill slyly.

Kimmick closed his mouth in a tight line and stared in front of him with his pale blue eyes fierce. Old Bill, satisfied that he'd won this round, walked away, saying to anyone who cared to listen, 'Well, I haven't got all day to hang about.'

'Mister,' I said to Kimmick. 'Do you reckon Hitler'll invade?'

Kimmick looked down at me. 'Well if he does, they won't stop him with a Lewis Gun,' and with that he marched off. A few minutes later the council men knocked off and the hole was left. That afternoon the rain came and the hole began to fill up with water. No one did anything with it for days, but the ropes stayed there and we had to go over to the other side of the rec to play football, which wasn't so good because the grass was longer. But we watched the roped-off space and hoped for excitement.

Next Saturday it came. There were soldiers in khaki jackets with bright brass buttons, peaked caps on their heads and puttees wound round their legs. And right in the middle of the roped-off ground, was the gun. To be honest, it wasn't all that marvellous: like a big fat rifle with a large round case stuck on top of it, all perched on a post which had been set up in the hole the council men had dug. Still, the soldiers looked real enough as they paced up and down around the gun, chasing off kids who ducked under the rope and tried to touch it.

Kimmick was there, chatting in familiar manner to a soldier with three stripes on his arm. I knew he must be a sergeant. Then I heard Old Bill's voice from the crowd.

'I don't see any Vickers Gun. Looks more like a Lewis to me.'

Kimmick took no notice.

Old Bill turned to one of his mates.

'Now if anyone was to ask you, Joe, wouldn't you say that looked distinctly like a Lewis Gun?'

Kimmick turned at last and said.

'Obviously it's a Lewis Gun, mounted for anti-aircraft purposes, the heavier weapon not being appropriate.'

'That's shut you up, Bill, hark to the voice of experience,' said Joe, grinning.

Kimmick turned his back and tried to carry on his conversation with the sergeant. But Old Bill spoiled it by saying :

'See you in the Red Lion, later, Sarge, I'll buy you one. You must be spitting feathers on this job.'

The sergeant grinned, but said nothing. The crowd started to break up. I ran back home along the Lane. I passed Harold and Bella's house and jumped up to look over the hedge, half hoping to see them. The Lewis Gun on the rec was important enough to make me call for them, but we hadn't been out together for weeks and I wasn't going to be first.

Over dinner I was full of the soldiers and the gun.

'They're expecting enemy planes over,' I said between mouthfuls. 'There's almost certain to be a war.'

To my surprise, Mam snapped:

'I'm sick and tired of your everlasting talk about war, war, war. Nobody wants a war.'

I felt my face go red, and went on with my meal. Nobody said any more and as soon as I could after dinner, I ran back to the rec. There were a handful of people there, standing by the ropes. The sergeant and the other soldiers had gone, leaving just one, a young, red-faced man, sweating in his tight tunic. He was getting more and more annoyed with kids nipping under the ropes, running across to touch the barrel of the gun and then ducking under the ropes on the other side.

At that moment up strolled Kimmick, followed by Old Bill and Joe. I think they'd been in the Red Lion. They weren't talking to one another, but at least they weren't falling out.

'Fancy a jar, mate?' Old Bill said to the man in khaki. Kimmick looked disapproving and the young soldier replied:

'Sarge'll have my guts for garters, if I do. But I could do with a cup of char – and a leak,' he added.

Joe spoke up. 'You can use our privy, lad. House with the green gate across the rec there. And knock on the kitchen door. Tell the missis I sent you, she'll mash you a can of tea.'

The young man shook his head. 'Daren't leave this. If one of these kids ...'

Kimmick cleared his throat.

'Not to worry, soldier. You get along. There's three

of us here can look after the old bundook, all long-service men. Go on.'

The soldier grinned and in a trice he was through the ropes and across the field, while Kimmick and the others stationed themselves inside the enclosure.

'Now then, lads,' Kimmick took charge. 'Let's have some action – ten paces back from those ropes.'

Reluctantly we moved back while the men clustered round the Lewis Gun, tapping it, pointing at various parts and nodding wisely. Old Bill familiarly tucked the butt of the gun into his shoulder and swung it in a wide arc. We all moved in closer to watch.

'Great old gun, this one,' he said.

Kimmick sniffed.

'All right for sticking on a post and pooping off at balloons. But useless for real action.'

'What? Talk sense man,' Bill shouted, sounding really offended. 'What d'you mean, useless?'

'Because they jam, that's what. That drum, it can't take the rapid fire.' He slapped the top of the magazine making the butt jump out of Bill's grip. We closed in now, hanging on the ropes. More kids came over from the other side of the rec. But Kimmick was so well into the argument now that he never noticed his ten paces rule was being broken.

Bill rounded on Kimmick, rubbing his jaw, which had received a smart tap from the gun butt.

'Jamming? Jamming? You don't know what you're talking about. This gun's for experts – not blaze-away-and-hope-you-hit-something wallahs. See.'

He snatched the butt from Kimmick's grasp and jerked it so that the barrel swung level, spun round and pointed direct at that gentleman.

'See, adaptability. Short, sharp bursts on a moving target.'

'Mind where you're pointing that,' yelled Kimmick, thrusting at the barrel, so that the post shook and the loose earth spurted up around the base.

'Who are you ordering about, mate?' snarled Bill, gripping the butt so that it pointed at Kimmick again. 'You never saw a Lewis Gun fired in anger in your life.'

'What, man? I was in action when you were digging chonnocks in your back garden,' growled Kimmick and lunged against the levelled barrel of the gun so that the post tilted.

'You gormless object, you'll have it off its mounting,' bellowed Old Bill, snatching the gun back so fiercely that the post rocked violently out of its upright position and leant crazily to the right.

'See what you've done now.' Kimmick grabbed Bill's arm and tried to drag him from the post. Bill resisted and the two wrestled together, the post and the gun bowing this way and that. Now Joe, who had been an interested spectator, joined the game, vainly trying to pull the two rival gunners apart. But in the confusion, matters went from bad to worse. We leaned on the ropes, waiting with pent-up breath for the whole issue to give way. But in the midst of it all, the young soldier, tea can in hand, came running across the field.

'What the hell d'you think you're doing, you maniacs,' he roared, ducking under the posts and rushing in among them.

For a moment it looked as though there might be a free for all, but the sound of his voice brought them to their senses. Joe steadied the gun barrel and Kimmick and Bill brought the post back to the upright position –

all three purple with excitement and embarrassment.

'I'll be for the high jump for this,' groaned the soldier.

'Get off, lad,' answered Joe. 'Look, I'll get a shovel from our shed. We'll have it back right as rain in two shakes. See,' and off he ran over the rec.

Kimmick, colour back to normal, turned and saw us hanging on the ropes with eyes wide and open mouthed.

'Sling your hook, you lot. You've no business here, messing about.' He made a move towards us and we scattered. As I turned I stumbled over the feet of someone who'd been in the crowd behind us. It was Bella. She grinned at me as we sloped off across the grass leaving the three musketeers busy with the Lewis Gun.

'I saw you going past the window,' she said. 'Why haven't you been round?'

'Well, you lot haven't called for me,' I answered sulkily.

'Mer,' she answered, 'Diddums.' Then she smiled and threw her arm over my neck.

'Coming home?'

I looked round. Tosher and the others had disappeared. I nodded. Bella and I trailed off along the road.

'Do you reckon there's going to be a war?' she asked. 'It'll be terrible, dropping bombs and gas and all on people.'

I nodded. 'My Mam reckons people who don't know anything about war, talk too much about it.'

'Oh ah. Hey, d'you think you'll get through the scholar this year?'

I shrugged. 'Search me.'

'They reckon, in the grammar, they put boys and girls at opposite ends of the school. They're not supposed to talk to each other.'

'Get off.'

'They do an' all. I heard it from a girl who's been there.'

'That's barmy, isn't it?'

'Well, it's what they do.'

We reached their gate.

'See you.'

'See you.'

I ran off home. We had jelly for tea.

That next week the wireless was talking about Mr Chamberlain and Munich. There wasn't going to be a war after all.

A week later, they'd taken the Lewis Gun away and filled in the hole and we were playing football again on the old patch. After a month or so we'd forgotten all about the gun and Old Kimmick and Bill and the caper they got up to.

Next year everything was changed. Bella and I went to the grammar – Harold was already there. Jammy and Tosher didn't, but I still saw them at weekends.

And the war came in the end. I heard it on the wireless and saw Mam put her handkerchief up to her eyes.

Later on, more soldiers came to the rec, dressed in khaki but rougher looking, no brass buttons and long puttees. They took over one corner of the field, by the woods, and built a proper place with a barbed wire fence, a gate and piles of sandbags. There was a big gun with a huge shiny metal barrel poking up in the sky, covered with camouflage netting.

Old Kimmick came and looked at it. But he didn't know what sort it was, until Jammy showed him a picture in a new book he had.

We had our own war now.

The Third Class Genie

ROBERT LEESON

Disasters were leading two nil on Alec's disaster-triumph
scorecard, when he slipped into the vacant factory lot,
locally known as the Tank. Ginger Wallace was hot on
his heels, ready to destroy him, and Alec had escaped just
in the nick of time. There were disasters awaiting him at
home too, when he discovered that he would have to move
out of his room and into the boxroom. And, of course,
there was school . . .

But Alec's luck changed when he found a beer can that
was still sealed, but obviously empty. Stranger still, when
he held it up to his ear, he could hear a faint snoring . . .
When Alec finally opened the mysterious can, something
happened that gave triumphs a roaring and most unexpected
lead.

A hilarious story for readers of ten upwards.

The Fib and other stories

GEORGE LAYTON

I was sick of Gordon Barraclough: sick of his bullying and his shouting, and his crawling round Mr Melrose, sick of him being a good footballer and going on about my old football gear. So I told him it had belonged to my uncle, who'd scored thousands of goals – because my uncle was Bobby Charlton! That was the fib. Then Bobby Charlton turned up as the surprise celebrity to switch on the Christmas lights outside the town hall. 'You're in for it now,' said Gordon, 'I told him you said he's your uncle.' I looked up at Bobby Charlton. He looked down at me. If only the earth would open and swallow me up . . .

Based on George Layton's own childhood, here are ten short, funny stories that come straight to the point on many important issues of adolescent life, such as school, girlfriends, football, and the problems of keeping in with your mates and getting round mum.